UPON ANOTHER EDGE BROKEN

ANTHONY W. EICHENLAUB

Print ISBN - 978-1-950542-10-9

Ebook ISBN - 978-1-950542-09-3

oakleafbooks.com

Cover Art by: Anthony W. Eichenlaub

❀ Created with Vellum

This book is dedicated to Bram Stoker, whose creepy weirdo thought so very highly of himself.

CHAPTER ONE

FAT DROPS of brown muck smacked granite like a downpour of bloated slugs. Upon the vast and rocky landscape of the planet Sky, the wet slapping rose to a roar and the air grew rank with the putrid scent of the muddy rain.

Nearly every person in the lonely mountaintop settlement of Edge agreed that the new, muddy rain was not a pleasant development. Not one bit. The precipitation reeked of the volatile organics of partially digested vegetation. Its texture resembled the slurry remaining when all but the most stubborn nutrients were removed from old foodstock. The slushy downpour was cold and filthy, covering the whole landscape with layer upon layer of grime.

"It's beautiful!" Ash Morgan shouted from atop a jagged boulder, spinning with her arms outstretched. Muddy rain sluiced off her wide-brimmed hat to dampen the ends of her shoulder-length hair.

Between her bright yellow slicker and galoshes that came up to her knees, she managed to keep herself fairly dry, despite the downpour. "This is biology at its best!"

Hector stood next to her with arms crossed. His black raincoat was a hooded thing and as simple as it gets, but elegantly functional just like its wearer. Hector's stated opinion, as it so often did, leaned dangerously close to the majority. "We're being crapped on." His big arms strained as he pulled his bigger belly atop the boulder.

Out over the endless ocean below, the sky disappeared into the muddy haze.

Ash said, "This is the biggest we've seen. Just like I predicted." She couldn't take notes easily in the rain, but she'd never had trouble memorizing observations.

"Didn't you also predict it would be blue?"

She grinned, feeling the bubbling, giddy sensation one gets in the presence of good, quality science. "There are variations."

"Brown isn't really a variation of blue, hon."

"It's just a little bit up the spectrum."

"People call this a crapstorm," Hector said. "Just so you know."

"They do not!"

He sniffed. "Smells about right."

"This isn't crap, and you know it. This is the depositing of a million million dead single-celled organisms. They're cleaning the air of poisonous particulates." Both Ash and Hector still wore their rebreathers—masks that allowed them to breath the air of Sky without suffering long-term consequences. Ash's itched, so she pulled off her rebreather and scratched the bridge of her nose, no doubt leaving a long smear of the brown sludge. The air *did* reek of methane and sulfur, but that really wasn't the point. It cleaned the atmosphere and brought Sky one step closer to habitability. "Ugh," she said, despite herself. Fine, it smelled terrible. Lots of science smelled terrible.

"See?" Hector said. "Now do you understand why people refuse to call it a blossom storm?"

Ash peered out into the heavy storm. "I admit it's fragrant."

"Fragrant isn't quite the right word, though, is it?"

Ash sat on the boulder that marked the halfway point between the quarry and the town, overlooking the small colony and the ocean beyond. As the storm intensified, even the colony itself became obscured. Soon, it was as if nothing else in the world existed except for her and Hector.

The stones were slick with the muddy rain, but she didn't mind. This was biology, and biology was gross sometimes. Hector sat next to her and put a big hand around her shoulders to pull her close. Despite the kind intent of his gesture, her nerves jangled like a bucket of broken beakers. Fear made her palms cold and her heart race. She looked away and tried her best to stifle the panic bubbling in her chest.

He must have noticed because he withdrew his hand.

"I'm sorry," she said as the sky brightened. They hadn't been any closer than that in all these months, and it hurt her knowing it was her fault, even if he always said it was fine.

"It's fine," Hector said.

Ash was tired of *fine*. Sick of it. Absolutely frustrated with it. "I'm sorry," she said again, so quiet she wasn't sure he could hear.

Above, through the mud-thick haze, something bright flashed in the sky. As the blossom storm ebbed, a pinpoint of blue-white light burned down to the mountains far away.

"Looks like a shuttle's headed for the other colony," Hector said. "I wonder if they're getting more people."

Ash's legs dangled over the edge. Far below, Edge sat atop the cliff over the ocean, but after a storm like this she couldn't see it at all. Edge once was the only colony on the planet Sky. When she had first discovered the second colony, it had been an empty husk awaiting colonists. Now that people started arriving, the place slowly woke to its own identity. She wondered how long it would be before they started developing their own biological fixes to the planet's many problems.

"We should visit them," she said.

"Ash."

"They could help us!"

"It's not allowed," Hector said, exhaustion apparent in his voice. They'd had this argument before, and as far as Ash was concerned, she always won.

Of course, she never got to actually *go* to the new colony, so maybe it was a draw. "Not allowed by Traverse," she said, trying a new angle, "the computer that almost killed us all over a silly technicality."

"The AI that still might kill us all over a silly technicality. Like the technicality that says it likes to keep its colonies apart. Or the technicality that it specifically *told* us not to interfere with the other colony and that if we did it might need to wipe us all out?"

"What about the technicality that we'd be really sneaky, and the stupid computer wouldn't even know anything?" There was a reason she had wanted to come so far from Traverse's sensors for their walk that morning. This far out, Traverse couldn't hear them talk. "With a fast enough walker, we could go there and back while the ship is below the horizon. It doesn't need to know."

"It's still a risk," Hector said, standing. He was a big man, with a belly that suited him well for long days sitting behind the controls of a spider walker in the construction fleet. "A big risk, and it risks everyone, not just you."

"They have tech we need," Ash said, pulling herself to her feet.

"No, they don't."

"They have skills we need. They still have most of our foodstock. We're struggling over here, and they've got a thousand people's worth of supplies and probably only a few hundred people. We could trade."

"We could die."

"There's a moderately good chance we wouldn't."

Tension hung between them, only to break when Ash swished her rain slicker and turned to the path back toward town. Hector, after a brief hesitation that could have been either deep sexual frustration or awe at Ash's superior arguing skills, followed. Ash spent the walk back trying to bring herself to hold his hand, but failed.

They reached the town as the first rays of morning sunlight hit the mud-drenched cobblestones through the clearing haze. An eerie quiet blanketed the little town. Nobody wandered outside, everyone having retreated to their homes or to work in order to avoid the glory of the glorious blossom storm. Ash walked through the empty streets, again reminded of the time she discovered the other colony all those months ago. It had been like walking into a ghost town, only everything there had been perfect and new, untouched by human hands. It had all been constructed by machines in preparation for a new wave of human inhabitants—inhabitants who now had been arriving for months and were uninformed about the dangerous unpredictability of their governing AI.

Hector was right, of course. The risk was too great. The colonies had to stay separate.

For now.

Her ankle twisted on the slick stone street, and Hector's big hand reached out to help. She took his arm in both of hers, and this time the fear didn't well up in her chest. Maybe she was recovering. Maybe the twisted trauma of that night months ago would finally fade from her heart.

And that was when she saw the dark heap on the street in front of the biolab.

Ash froze, her heart hammering in her chest. Her hands went cold. Hector made a frustrated noise and pulled his arm away, but she ignored him.

Instinct told her this was that day all over again. The storm, the death. She relived the entire lightning storm in her head over and over again, and here it was, the results right in front of her, face down in the freshly fallen mud.

Hector, oblivious, talked next to her, telling her all about his plans for the Landingday Festival.

"Ash!" Olympia called from around the corner of the lab. "Karl's pissed at you, girl."

Ash turned to where her curvy and gorgeous lab partner emerged from a wing of the biolab. Olympia's dreadlocks were scooped up behind her in a simple, easy-to-manage arrangement. She wore uncharacter-istically baggy scrubs, and her face was a shade paler than usual, likely an effect of the blossom storm's all-encompassing fragrance.

From her vantage point, Olympia couldn't see the shape in the middle of the street, and Ash didn't want to be the one to tell her of its existence. How could she be the person to make this real for her friend?

But that was stupid and Ash knew it. From where she stood, she couldn't say for certain what lay in the street. What if it was just a duffel someone had left while fleeing from the storm? A duffel with boots.

And glossy black hair.

"Why?" Ash managed to say, not knowing exactly what she was asking.

"He's still upset that you broke safety protocols and unleashed this nasty mess." Olympia peered up at the sky, testing the air with an open palm before stepping out from under the overhang. "Never mind that your crapstorms move this planet one step closer to being truly habitable. We're changing the world, you know? Makes sense that the older colonists might be a little jealous. Ash, what is wrong with you? Are you even listening?"

Ash managed to point at the heap in the street. She couldn't breathe.

Olympia narrowed her eyes, still not in a position to see what Ash was pointing at. She took a step forward out of the lab's entryway. Then another.

Finally, Hector saw what Ash had seen under the layers of muck. Leaving Ash to her stunned silence, he rushed to where it lay.

When he flinched back like he'd been bit, Ash

knew that her first instinct was correct. It was a body. A body left out in the middle of a storm.

Olympia covered her mouth with one hand. With her other, she pulled Ash close. "Oh no," she said. "Oh no, oh no."

Hector looked up, eyes wide. "It's Paige Liu. She's dead."

CHAPTER TWO

DELILAH BAXTER ARRIVED like a storm cloud on a sunny afternoon. Her brown tweed suit sported synthetic leather elbow pads and real carved wooden buttons. Her glasses employed a kind of trifocal lens that fractured her eyes when viewed straight on, but gave her the appearance of an aloof attitude whenever she read, as if the screen she was reading had best recognize that she was one of the colony's original inhabitants and as such demanded the utmost respect. Even her rebreather had class, with an ornate frill along the frowning corners of its downturned form.

Del, as she preferred, headed the Edge Volunteer Interventions Committee. Ash normally found the middle-aged woman to be gruff and unapproachable, despite the woman's impeccable fashion sense. She tried to avoid her at all costs, all the time, no matter what.

"You'll want fingerprints," Ash said as Del peered at the body. "And you'll want to test for DNA residue."

Without looking up, Del said, "Are you volunteering?"

"No."

"But you consider yourself the expert."

"I've spent thousands of hours watching education videos regarding forensic science and the investigative process." She neglected to mention that her source was mostly Earth-based entertainment media.

"Good."

"Good?"

"I was hoping for a volunteer and I'm glad to have found one."

"But I said I didn't volunteer."

Del looked up from her analysis and fixed Ash with a gaze so unrelenting it hurt. "Did you?"

Ash swallowed the lump in her throat. "I'm really better at telling you how to do your job."

"Start with sequencing the DNA."

"I can run a full analysis."

"No need. Just get me the DNA and get back to your regular job for now." She started walking the perimeter of the crime scene. "We all have our work, Miss Morgan, and I'm sure they miss you at the lab." She cast a meaningful look at the crowd gathering outside the lab. "I'm sure Karl is missing a lot of people right now." She shot Hector a meaningful look.

Hector corralled the group, keeping them a good twenty yards away from where Paige Liu still lay face down in the muck. They watched with somber expressions on their faces. Ash recognized them all. It wasn't a large colony. She knew everyone. Could one of them be the killer?

One of them *had* to be the killer.

"How do you know it's a murder?" Ash stepped forward.

Hector said, "Ash." His voice rang with warning.

Ash hated that tone. Curiosity drove her another step forward. "The body isn't covered in a thick layer of blooms," she said. "So, it must have happened late in the blossom storm."

"Excuse me?" Del said. "The blossom what?"

"Storm. When the atmospheric cleansers bloom, they fall to the earth. It's how they remove particulates from the air and—"

"I haven't heard it called that."

Ash frowned. "That's what everyone calls it."

Del humphed. Having circled the corpse, she closed in, making a point of showing off her technique for recording and observing everything about the body and its surroundings. She took careful notes on a handheld screen and verified with Hector when she wasn't sure if a footprint belonged to him. The patience and thoroughness of the process made Ash antsy.

"Miss Morgan," Del said. "Are you going to help or not?"

Ash's mouth ran dry, but she said, "I thought you wanted me to run a DNA scan."

"Are you doing that right now?"

"No."

"Good. Come help me move this body."

"Body?"

"The dead one."

Ash approached Paige's corpse. It made her nervous, lying there like it might be any old object right on the street, with its matte of black hair sprawled about its face and its bruised, broken limbs cast at odd angles. The gorge rose in Ash's stomach, but she hadn't gotten into microbiology without learning a thing or two about fighting nausea.

Ash had only ever seen one other corpse, and that was Marta. The dead on the space station Traverse where she grew up were handled coolly and efficiently by machines. Maybe too efficiently. For generations, Traverse whisked away bodies and pretended like the people had simply moved to another borough. Falsified videoconferences convinced friends and family that their loved ones still lived. This was why Ash and the colonists feared the AI. If it could manage such a willful and wicked deception in the name of efficiency, what else could it do? What lies did they still believe?

Heart pounding in her throat, Ash bent down close to the corpse. "It was supposed to be blue," she said, unsure why her brain insisted that she say something.

"Excuse me?"

"The blossom storm. My simulations indicated that it would be blue."

Del blinked rapidly several times. "You're right about the corpse. If she were killed before the storm, she would have been covered completely. She only has a thin layer, so that gives us a decent estimate of the time of death."

Ash swallowed the realization. "She must have been killed moments before Hector and I arrived."

"Not necessarily." Del took hold of Paige's legs. "Help me here."

"I have to touch her?"

"We need to roll her over onto her back."

Ash, trembling, touched the body, taking the woman's shoulders and rolling her to one side with Del's help. Paige's empty eyes pointed at the gray sky above. Or, rather, her one blank eye. Singular. Ash gasped and stumbled back.

Paige's face had been slashed to the bone, ruining one eye and splitting her nose and lips in two. Her simple gray scrubs, the kind biolab workers often wore during their days in the lab, were splattered with blood and muck. Too much muck. Ash's brain grasped for facts that might be relevant, because otherwise all she could think about was poor Paige.

Poor, kind Paige.

"She was in the storm," Ash said. "Part of it, anyway."

Del chewed her lip. "The blood shows she was

cut after being in the storm. Blood layered atop muck. She must have been killed here."

"All right, people," Hector shouted to the crowd. "Show's over, let's move out."

Del leaned close to Ash and winked. "He's a good one you got there, but I don't think he's got the pull to get people to actually leave."

"I'm not sure I've got him at all," Ash said. "It's complicated."

The older woman nodded at this response. She used several vials to gather samples from various places on the body and ground.

Ash stood, taking a step back from the corpse. A med tech whose name she couldn't remember stood next to her with a folded stretcher and a long piece of dark cloth.

"Perfect," Del said. "Get the body into storage and I'll look more closely at it later. Ash, check these samples for any DNA that doesn't belong to you, me, Hector, or Paige."

"But Karl—"

"Can go shove it."

Ash's mouth worked, but no more words came. She looked down at the body as the techs covered Paige's horrific face. The thought of seeing it again sent a shudder down her spine. She remembered Marta's death, how the woman had gone insane and been struck by lightning in that horrible storm. Her body had been ruined from the lightning and the fall, and Ash blamed herself for it.

The nightmares had almost stopped, and now this.

And yet.

She remembered the stories from Earth. The books she'd read on her long time aboard the ship and the shows she had watched. She remembered the excitement of discovery and the thrill of uncovering a clue mere seconds before the mystery's true reveal. She thought of the fantastic things that detectives discovered and how they could root the darkest evils out of society. Maybe finding Paige's killer would give her an opportunity to make the colony a better place.

"All right," Ash said, but Del wasn't listening. She'd gone with the med techs and the body, and the crowd lost its cohesion. Ash stood holding the vials. "All right."

The biology lab, which Ash had always considered her very own extra special lab where all the smart stuff happened, had several entrances. She picked the least traveled of them, not because she was intentionally avoiding Karl, but because she needed to change out of the yellow rain slicker, which was far too cheery for her current mood. Also, it still dripped with muck, and she couldn't stand it anymore, even if the muck happened to be the proper functioning of her own biological creation.

Once inside, she placed her vials, one by one, in a proper carrier. It wouldn't do to drop them all over the floor, not that the non-reactive synthetic substance would likely break. She arranged them by color, because that seemed appropriate. On one end, the contents were brown and watery, while on the other they were thick red blood. Paige's blood.

As much as it pained her, Ash picked up the gray scrubs of a biology technician. Her muck-covered clothes went into the material recycler, to be processed into whatever the next person wanted to make—probably plain gray scrubs, those monsters. She came back out after showering and dressing to find Karl Planski peering at her colorful row of vials.

"You'll want help with this," he said, peering at the last vial. "So you don't fall behind in your other work."

Karl Planski was a mean old man. He stood no taller than Ash and his steely hair stuck out at odd, presumably unplanned angles. This would never have bothered Ash, except that he had something seriously against her that she couldn't quite figure out.

"Someone will need to shadow you to make sure you follow safety protocols," he said.

Really. No idea why at all.

When she didn't respond, he narrowed his eyes. "This is a murder investigation, not some world-altering biosynth that you can just release with hardly any testing."

Nope. She probably never would figure it out. "I'm fine," she said. "I'll follow protocol." After releasing her spores into the atmosphere, Karl had demoted her. She no longer got to run her own experiments. In fact, she hardly ever got to actually help with any proper science. If Olympia hadn't been feeding her interesting tidbits of work, she'd be stuck titrating random liquids all day long.

Karl squinted at her. "You'll be expected to continue your regular duties."

"But Del said—"

"Delilah Baxter doesn't run this lab, and she never will."

"Olympia will help me."

"What if she's the killer."

"She can't be."

Karl lowered his voice, speaking with something resembling compassion. "Did you witness her not murder Paige?"

Ash shook her head. "She wouldn't do it. I *know* her."

Karl placed a hand on Ash's arm, and Ash tried her best not to go defensively tense. "There was a time when I'd have claimed that of every person in this colony. I would have vouched for every single one of them and sworn up and down that we must be dealing with killer robots or some kind of madness." He gave her arm a squeeze and then let go. "That time was yesterday, Ash. We're all coming to terms with this."

Ash tried to keep the emotion from shaking her voice. "Olympia wouldn't do it."

Karl's voice turned hard. "This still doesn't get you out of your regular duties."

Picking up her vials and leaving, Ash muttered to herself, "Those liquids aren't going to just titrate themselves, are they?"

Olympia's lab station sat right next to Ash's old one. The old station now seated Leonard, who wasn't even really a biologist. Ash ran a hand along the churning fabrication unit, which she had once used to create life. Leonard used it to create pointless distractions. The assignment was probably meant as an insult to her genius, but she wasn't about to let it get to her.

She flicked a rock sample off the top of the display box, pelting Leonard in the face. "Jerk."

"Please leave me alone, Ash," he said, as if his work were somehow that important. "I'm very busy."

She sighed and set down her vial holder at Olympia's station. Olympia wasn't back yet, probably taking some time off to process the events of the day. Ash wished she had the luxury. Why had she said anything to Del?

"Traverse," she said to the computer, "I need some music. Something somber and very serious."

Traverse's neon green T logo spun for several seconds before a low rich melody rolled out through the speakers. A cello, Ash knew. Something old.

"Thanks."

Leonard sighed loudly and put on a pair of headphones.

Karl made it sound like her investigation might take some time, but really there wasn't much to it.

The vials Del used were a machine standard variety. Ash didn't even need to open them up in order to feed them into full analysis. Traverse would run every test in the book, come up with gene sequencing for every living or formerly living tissue in the sample, and give a full chemical analysis complete with an isotope breakdown. It was absolutely everything they would need for a proper forensic investigation. Ash's research of Earth media even told her it was exactly what police expected in the old days.

All Ash needed to do was trust the machine—the machine that managed the colony's resources, kept them alive every single day, predicted the weather, and—

And killed her parents for population control. She took a set of fresh syringes and drew a small sample from each vial. Using the bioprinter, she printed a suitable substitute for paper and a bright-yellow graphite pencil, so that no notes she took would show in the system. Labeling each syringe with a letter, she wrote on the paper where each one came from and what it represented. There were five. One of the muck some distance from Paige's body, one mixed with water and blood from next to her corpse, one from atop the body, one from underneath, and one that was a pure sample of her blood. They were unlikely to hold anything useful. Ash knew that anything anywhere might hold a fragment of a colonist's DNA. It only meant close contact, it didn't point to murder.

Still, she wanted to know everything the samples showed.

"Traverse," she said, "run a full analysis on these samples." She entered the information for the vials into the computer, making sure everything lined up correctly. "When it's finished, let me know."

The logo spun for several seconds. When the ship high above the atmosphere dipped below the horizon, Traverse took longer to perform calculations. This was one of those times. "Affirmative."

"Whatcha doing?" Olympia said behind her, startling Ash right the heck out of her loose-fitting pants. The woman was Ash's lab station partner, quasi-boss, and longtime friend, but still intimidating as hell.

"Investigating," Ash said.

Olympia sauntered around so she could see the screen. Her dark skin still looked a shade too pale to Ash, but the green light from the screen could do that. The scent of cinnamon hung in the air around the woman. "Full scan? With paragenetic analysis?"

"That's right."

"Using my ID?"

Ash peered at the screen. "Maybe." Yes. She had done everything signed in as her partner. Really, Olympia shouldn't be leaving her station logged in when she left, but it was Ash's fault for not checking. Luckily, Olympia was pretty cool about that kind of thing. "Del only wanted a DNA sequencing, but you get that with a full scan."

"Ash," she said, exasperated. "Karl constantly

checks the activity logs. This isn't like when you used my ID to design that weapons-grade chocolate. He almost believed that I'd been working on that as a side project."

"Tell him it's a lady thing."

"I did. The point is, he already knows you're the one working with Del on this... this accident."

"Murder."

She let out a small puff of air. "Yeah."

"Do you want me to cancel and relog as myself?"

"No," she said. "Leave it. I'll explain to Karl that we're teaming up on this and used my ID so that we didn't need to worry about authority."

"Thanks."

Olympia waved dismissively, as if she couldn't be bothered to deal with whatever it was Ash had going on. This might have been normal for Olympia, but something about her reaction seemed off. It was too much. Too performative. Either way, the scan started, and according to Karl, Ash had work to do. The answers would come on their own, and if they didn't she still had the backup samples.

Ash pulled out a tray of liquids and started the long slow job of titrating the hell out of them.

CHAPTER THREE

Ash found Leonard eating lunch on a recently cleaned bench outside the northern side of the biolab, so she sat next to him, even though he was a serious jerk for stealing her lab station. He was a heavyset man with exploding gray hair whose eyes always asked a question through a flimsy pair of bent glasses.

She pulled a ham sandwich out of her cooler, unwrapped it from its wax paper packaging, and took a bite.

"Was it you?" she asked through a mouthful of crumbling, dry bread.

"Pardon?" Leonard spoke as if he'd just noticed her, but she knew he'd seen her. He wasn't *that* oblivious.

"Just seeing how you'd react."

"React to what?" He gripped his sandwich with the scarred, calloused fingers of a less-than-careful chemist. The meat wasn't ham, but Ash couldn't tell what kind it was. The stuff all came from the same food printer anyway, so it was largely a matter of coloring.

"I was just wondering what your thoughts were about the thing this morning."

"Did they announce the Landingday color themes?" The Landingday Festival was the biggest yearly event on the entire planet, and some people got really worked up about it. Up close, Ash could see the bags under Leonard's eyes, which indicated he might be one such person.

"What are you doing for festival prep?" she asked.

"Fireworks and other chemical-related enter-tainment."

Ash didn't have any idea why anyone would care about non-firework chemical entertainment, but whatever. "So, you were at your lab all morning?"

"I split time between my lab station and the storage facility."

"Where's that?"

A thunder of activity rumbled from up the street, and a spider walker plodded along the cobblestones, scouring everything in sight with a seriously overpow-ered washer. Water sluiced down the ruts as it cleaned the results of the morning's storm. Ash spotted Hector driving the spider and waved, but he probably didn't see her because he didn't wave back.

When the noise died down, Ash said, "Doesn't that waste water?"

"There's a whole reservoir and last I heard it was pretty full. They don't even need to use filtered stuff for this kind of work."

Ash remembered the work Olympia had been doing on designing new filters and the hollowed-out look on her face. Poor, overworked Olympia, toiling extra hours because of Ash's blossom storms. "It just seems like a waste of water."

"Maybe that's something that should have been considered before unleashing your scrubbers into the world."

Desperate for a change in subject, Ash said, "Paige is dead."

Leonard dropped his sandwich. The bread broke to pieces when it struck the floor. He turned on her, his face red and his jaw loose. It was exactly the kind of expression she expected from someone pretending to learn about a murder for the first time. He rushed back into the lab.

Ash crammed the remains of her sandwich into her face. When she returned to the lab, she ran head-long into Morton, the janitor, outside Karl's office. "Sorry!"

"Oh no," Morton said. He had speckled gray hair and a coarse beard that almost covered the pockmarks on the left side of his face. "I'm the one who's sorry, Miss Morgan."

She couldn't imagine why he would be sorry. "It's just, I need to get back to work."

"Same here." Morton flashed a bright smile and

patted the garbage cart that he was pulling from Karl's oversized office. Karl's status as head of the lab granted him a huge space to do his work, and the man had done shockingly little with the space. The wall shelves stood empty and the lab space was shockingly neat.

Ash reached past Morton to hit the wall controls for the light. "Karl hates coming back and finding his lights on."

Morton tipped an imaginary hat. "Thanks." He pointed down the hall at the farthest science stations. "Best not to be on his bad side right now. Those two are at it again."

Olympia and Karl argued with barely contained fury right in front of Olympia's lab station, so Ash veered away to check on her other project. She'd set the fiber printer to make a new set of scrubs for her, and it had just finished. Pulling the hot-pink garments on, she finally felt her mood lift a little. Who can go around wearing gray all day, anyway? Well, except for Olympia. She managed to make even the dullest colors look fantastic.

She stepped out of the changing room to find Del waiting with her arms crossed. "Ash," the older woman said.

Across the hall, Morton watched the two of them for a long, awkward second, then moved on his way.

"Why do I keep getting ambushed here?" Ash said.

"I need the results of that DNA test."

"This takes time, you know."

Del's lips pressed into a thin line. "I need something else too."

"I've watched a million hours of media about investigations. Hit me."

"I need you to question people in the lab. Discreetly, if possible. I want to know if anyone is acting suspicious or if anyone noticed anything out of the ordinary. Or saw anyone they didn't recognize."

Edge wasn't very big. Ash recognized every person in the entire town—and by extension, almost every person on the entire planet. If there might be another person around, then they must have come from outside, and that meant Del suspected someone from the other colony. "What did you find?" she asked the investigator. "Did surveillance video pick something up?"

"Everything outside was covered in mud. Half the cameras in the lab have been wiped."

"Wiped?" Ash blinked.

"Erased."

That meant someone in the lab could have been involved. "Can you recover anything?"

"Just find out where everyone was during the killing and that'll be a big help." She handed Ash a sleek baton made of dense carbon fiber. "Clip this to your belt."

"Am I supposed to rough people up?"

"Only if you're pretty sure they're a murderer."

Ash stuck her head around the corner and peered

at the rows of lab stations. Dozens of scientists worked in the lab, and Ash knew every one of them. Morton strolled from station to station, smiling kindly at each of the scientists. "They couldn't have killed anyone, Del."

Del's expression went flat. "You'd be surprised at who is and isn't capable of murder, Ash."

"These are people dedicated to helping this world." She chewed her lip. "We *create* life here. We don't end it." She thought about it for a moment. "Except for Leonard. He creates fireworks."

"*Someone* murdered Paige. If a struggle started here in the lab, then there's limited access and our search can be narrowed. If it happened outside, it could be anyone."

"I can't think of anyone who might kill Paige."

"We don't have the luxury to pretend like it didn't happen."

Ash crossed her arms. Del was right. "I already talked to Leonard."

"Great. Did he see anything?"

"I don't know."

"Was he with anyone? Does he have an alibi?"

"Um..."

"Ash." Del's tone was disapproving.

"He dodged my questions! Isn't that a sign of guilt?"

Del pinched the bridge of her nose. "Take a notepad and collect as many statements as you can." With that she left to go do super important investigator activities that Ash imagined probably involved coffee and a gigantic corkboard.

Ash peeked around the corner again. Olympia and Karl had retreated from their battle in front of the lab station, so she went to check on her analysis. Still incomplete. No progress indicator.

"Traverse, how long will this take?"

"Unknown."

Ash let out a loud sigh. She took her notepad from the stack, retrieved her bright yellow pencil, and started making the rounds of the biolab.

"Skyarrhea," Jasper told her. He was a tall thin man a few years older than Ash and apparently considered himself quite clever, even though he most definitely was not. He wore the standard gray scrubs of a biologist, but he had printed the pants too short so that his distractingly curly leg hairs waved in the upward draft of the vent hood surrounding his station. "You know, like diarrhea."

"Yeah, I get it, Jasper. Don't call it that."

"Why not?"

"Then everyone will call it that and nobody will realize how beautiful the blossom storm really is."

"It's watery poop raining from the sky."

"All biology is beautiful."

"You should go say that to Gerald. I'm sure he'd love to hear it."

"What's Gerald working on?"

"Bugs, these days, I think, and he refuses to dispose of anything he creates." Jasper pinched the bridge of his nose with his gloved hands. "Anyway, I wasn't in the lab this morning. I got a late start, and I don't like walking through—blossom storms."

"Were you with anyone?"

"Juliette was with me."

"Really? Juliette from Food Processing?"

Jasper gave Ash a dry look. "Don't be so surprised, Ash. She's older than me, but not by that much."

"I thought she had better taste."

"Ha ha."

"Pooicane," said Cynthia as she carefully loaded a rack of printed cell starters into the incubator. She was a heavyset woman who wore scrubs so old the gray cloth had frayed around the edges. Her short-cropped hair showed hints of amber, which contrasted against her dark skin.

"If you're mixing poop and hurricane you're implying wind speeds that weren't really present."

"Yeah," said Cynthia, "but there was enough precipitation that a poo-drizzle didn't quite handle it."

"Poo-drizzle doesn't have a ring to it at all." Ash wrote *pooicane* on her notepad under the Cynthia heading.

"That's true too." Cynthia crossed her arms and fixed Ash with narrow, suspicious eyes.

"Some people are calling it a blossom storm, because it's the microbe blossoming that causes the weather effect."

"Uh-huh."

"Either way, you missed the storm?"

"I was here really early this morning. I had extra work to do to get ready for Landingday."

Ash made a note of that. "Who else did you see here at the time?"

"Well, I was working alone back in this wing, so I didn't really talk with anyone. Olympia and Leonard were both here. Arguing. Flirting, maybe. Olympia kept making trips to the bathroom."

"Isn't Olympia with Simon?"

"I don't think that one was destined to last."

"How could you tell?" Ash chewed her pencil's eraser. It wasn't really an eraser, just a differently colored nub on the end of the pencil.

"It's pretty common for couples who get together in a stressful situation to break up shortly after. They started dating right around the time of that thing with the weird baby."

"Skye?"

"Yeah. Olympia had strong opinions about that. He had differently strong opinions. That's just the way it goes."

Ash was friends with both Simon and Olympia and hadn't heard anything about either of their strong opinions. "Anybody else around that morning?"

"Karl's always here, so there's that. I saw Paige when I came in, but she was packing her things up to leave. She seemed upset."

"What time was that?"

Cynthia chewed her lip. "Around the time the sky started getting really brown. I didn't really check the time. You could probably get the weather report from Traverse."

Ash wanted to say that Traverse's logs might be unreliable, but she held back. That wasn't really the point of the interview, and anyway why would Traverse want to manipulate the results of the weather records? "Were you at your station the whole time?"

"No. I needed to go back and forth to get more substrate. Karl's not letting us withdraw large quantities now that supplies are so low, so I needed to visit the big recycler outside to recycle what I had going from last week's project."

"What project was that?"

"Olympia gave me the recipe for some really top-notch chocolate."

"What?" Ash set down her pencil and paper. "She *gave* that to you?"

"It wasn't very good. There was something wrong with the chemical balance."

Ash wrote down in her notes that Cynthia might be the killer, and that she was starting to have doubts about Olympia as well. Why would her friend and lab partner steal her weapons-grade chocolate recipe and give it to Cynthia? Plus, anyone who didn't like good chocolate was likely the kind of sociopath who might murder a fellow biolab employee just for the thrill of it. At least Ash's extensive research on the topic indicated that might be true. Earth entertainment media mostly ignored the existence of printable chocolate.

"Precrapitation," said Gerald without looking up from his display. Green light from the screen shone against pale skin creased with age and filtered through his greasy black hair to reflect against narrow wire frame glasses. A model of a winged insect spun as he tweaked a complex DNA sequence, and he flinched every time the machine ran another calculation. "It's a—"

"Yeah, I get it. Did you kill anyone this morning?"

Gerald sputtered coffee all over the front of his boring gray scrubs. His dark eyes searched her features.

"Just answer the question, chump."

"Life is sacred to me." When he saw that the answer didn't satisfy her, he added, "I have never killed anyone."

Ash made a note. The interviews weren't very productive, and she'd wasted too much time on them. There was titrating to be done, after all, and she wasn't going to win back Karl's trust anytime this decade, especially if she kept distracting the other lab techs.

"I did see someone outside, though," Gerald said.

"During the storm?"

"Toward the end, when it wasn't so, um, dungy outside." He swept his black hair to one side as he spoke, and Ash caught a look of fear in his eyes.

When he spoke again, it was a harsh whisper. "There was something at the window."

"Something?"

Gerald twitched. He hunched over his console so she couldn't see and pressed in his security passcode. A section of the wall slid out to reveal a honeycomb of terrariums, each containing a mix of substrate, water, and egg clusters. "Someone," he muttered. "Someone."

"Who?"

He gestured to the window twenty feet away. "Right out there, in the hardest downpour. But when I looked out the window, it—he—had moved. I saw a figure downhill along the outskirt road. I thought it was strange anyone would be out there during a storm."

Ash pressed her pencil to her lips. "Doesn't seem so strange in itself."

He gestured wildly. "It was raining crap from the sky, Ash. Who would willingly go out in that?"

"Maybe they had a good appreciation of the biological processes involved."

Gerald stared at her, his face a carefully controlled lack of expression. He whispered, "You were out there, weren't you?"

"Hector wanted to see it."

A wide grin crossed his narrow face. "I guarantee he did not."

"We were up by the quarry and came back

through the northern road. Are you sure it wasn't us you saw?"

"No, I'm positive. The beast I saw ran past the pipe rocks. You know, down where those skinny lava tubes come out?"

"Beast?"

"Person, I said." He studied his terrariums very closely. He slid another section of the wall out to reveal a row of slimy blue, green, and yellow creatures with webbed feet. "I said person."

"They're very pretty," Ash said, nodding at the creatures. "Are those frogs?"

"The lava tubes," he said. "It was down by the lava tubes."

She wrote a *maybe* next to Gerald's name. "Thanks for your help."

"Does *maybe* mean I might be the killer?" he said, peering at her notes.

Ash pressed her notebook to her chest to hide what she'd written there. "It's in code," she said. It was not.

"I didn't kill anyone, Ash. The lost life force—" he cut himself off. "I don't think anyone here ever could kill anyone."

"We don't have the luxury of pretending like it didn't happen." She walked to the window where Gerald said he had seen a beast. Outside, Morton's arms shook as he tipped the cart into the steel chute on the side of a machine. Ash made a mental note to scrape the logs to find out what he was throwing away. "Was it out there by the bulk recycler?"

"Yes," Gerald said. "When I first saw it."

"Then it was down by the tubes? How did it get there so fast?"

"Maybe it flew."

"Thanks, Gerald."

With that, Ash returned to her own lab station where Olympia toiled at the latest chemical-filtering simulation. The screen glitched and spun, showing upside-down letters and squiggly marks where it ought to have had numbers. It had been a while since Traverse had exhibited the problems to this degree, but they were always present.

Ash's titration setup sat untouched, ready for hours of mindless drudgery.

"Any leads?" Olympia asked without looking up from her work.

Ash's notebook listed the names of everyone working in the lab. Next to every name was the word *maybe*, except for Gerald where the word was scratched out and replaced with a *probably*. It wasn't helpful.

"One," Ash said.

Olympia stopped her work. "Really?"

"I uncovered some serious criminal activity."

"Is it Morton?"

"He's giving you trouble again?"

Olympia scrunched up her nose. "Flirting,

mostly. Keeps offering to help me get Karl off my back, as if I need any help with that."

"That doesn't sound like a crime."

"What terrible crimes did you come up with in your investigation?"

"Theft. Of private information. One chocolate recipe."

Olympia didn't respond for a while, making a pretty good show of being absorbed in her super important work on the filtration system. When she finally spoke, a thread of annoyance tightened around her words. "I suppose you better send in that report before you get back to work."

"Hey," Ash said, "have you been feeling all right?"

Olympia's perfect lips tightened into a line. For a split second, Ash thought she saw something relent behind the beautiful woman's dark eyes, but then Olympia turned back to her work and said, "I've been busy."

It was late afternoon when Ash stepped out of the biolab. The blue sun shone down on the newly cleaned streets, but the stench of the blossom storm still lingered in the humid air. Ash hesitated to don her rebreather. Immediately following the storm, the air was clean and pure. Well, as clean and pure as it could possibly be after raining brown muck.

From her place on the steps of the biolab, she could see down the slope to the south where the narrow lava tubes jutted from black rock. Hector and his crew hadn't yet cleaned that area. It still bore the brown slime coating of the morning's storm, but another storm brewed in the eastern sky. Brown clouds rolled closer in an enormous wall, ready to slam into the colony at full force and cover the world in another layer of muck, erasing all the cleaning that Hector had done throughout the day.

Erasing any footprints formed in muck after the morning's storm.

And the next storm was coming fast.

Ash ran down the slope.

CHAPTER FOUR

"I THOUGHT THE BACK WAS HOLLOW," Ash said, peering at Hector's big black spider walker.

"That's the construction model. This is the cleaning version. One of its front legs shoots clean water, the other sucks up muck and water. All that liquid gets stored in the back."

"So, I'll have to ride in the front seat with you."

He shook his head. "It's too cramped."

Ash bit back a retort. It had worked before, but maybe he didn't want to be that close anymore. Or, maybe he figured *she* didn't want to be that close. Fair enough. "I can ride on top."

He closed his eyes for several long seconds. The tension of his long days at work was wearing on him; she could see it in the tightness of his jaw and his hunched shoulders.

"Please?" she asked.

"Climb up."

He only let her struggle for a few excruciating seconds because Hector was a true gentleman. When, finally, he helped, Ash felt the strength in his big hands as he lifted her up, and it hardly triggered her panic reflex at all.

The spider didn't offer a smooth ride, but Ash clung to the top and learned to shift her weight with every swaying movement. Hector maneuvered the machine down to the lava tubes and lowered it so she could hop to the ground.

"It's over here," she shouted, unsure if he could hear her from inside the spider's pilot cabin.

The trail wound its way out of town along a path strewn with shards of jet-black obsidian and lined with the thin lava tubes that snaked their way up toward the blue-gray sky. She'd easily spotted the footprints when she first came down, pausing for ten minutes to run and get Hector—a move that she now considered to be very smart, even though it had taken at least twenty minutes. Half an hour, really, since she needed a change of clothes. She couldn't go tracking killers without a decent pair of cargo pants and a windbreaker that said "POLICE" in big yellow letters on the back. It wouldn't be proper.

And now, the trail had changed. Another set of prints ran along the lower ridge. She waved for the spider to follow, and ran down the trail, her galoshes barely slipping on the muck-slick stone.

"Ash," said a voice up ahead.

Ash stopped. "Del?" She made her way forward

across a razor-sharp ridge of glassy black rock, careful not to let her bare skin touch the jagged stone. "What are you doing here?"

Del's voice was dry. "Same as you, I figure." She stepped out from behind a row of tubes. "Looking for the scene of the murder."

"Gerald told me he saw someone down here."

Del nodded at the tracks. "Gerald's always been a little unhinged, but he probably wasn't lying." She grinned when Hector's street-cleaner rounded the corner. "Good thinking, kid. If we catch the murderer, we can give them a good washing."

"Climb up," Ash said, "and we can track the killer from our luxurious ride."

Del's expression was skeptical, but she scrambled up without any help at all from Hector. From atop the spider, she and Ash could easily see where someone had climbed a series of boulders to circle west around the settlement. Ash pounded on the side of the spider and Hector walked the machine forward and up the slope.

After they had traveled a fair distance, Del said, "You shouldn't say that, you know."

"What?"

"That we're following the killer."

"I thought you said the murder scene was out here."

"Based on analysis of the wound, the murder weapon contained flecks of burgundy obsidian."

"Isn't obsidian black?"

Del gestured at the ground. "Everything I found here was pure black. Burgundy obsidian has a reddish swirl in it, and it's rare. Paige was bludgeoned as well as cut. Seems likely that the murderer could have picked up a stray rock and used it in a moment of passion, but the question is where."

"I thought she was killed near the lab."

"Maybe."

"Well, all I care about is who."

Del nodded. "That's an interesting question, yes, but there's more to it than that. Why would someone kill Paige? Answering the questions of where and how might give us clues to that. The kind of wound hints at a deeply personal motive. Once we have all of that answered, the question of who should be trivial."

"I've seen enough mysteries to understand motives and opportunities."

"Have you? Do you really know how murder investigations work? I sure don't." Del gave her a hard look, broken only when the spider mounted a particularly difficult rise. "And I'm the expert on the subject."

The going became steep, and Ash wondered how their quarry even managed to climb this way without the aid of a machine. When she looked, however, the person's footprints and sometimes handprints were apparent along the ridges of rock. "It's an adult," she said. "Probably male, based on the size of the boots, and he must be in decent shape."

"It'd be hard to make it all this way," Del agreed. "But why come this way at all? All we've done so far is make a wide circle around Edge."

Ash sat for a long time, watching the sky and the terrain. The sun neared the horizon as they rode the spider to the west across the rugged land. "We're headed toward the other colony."

"He wouldn't run there, would he?" A hint of fear crept into Del's voice. "Everyone knows the risk."

"Maybe he figures it's his only chance at escape."

Del shook her head. "That makes no sense. Traverse might kill all of us as soon as contact is made."

Ash swallowed the lump in her throat. "That's what Hector thinks too." She tried to keep the bitterness from her voice, but might have failed terribly.

"He's right," Del said.

"He usually is." Ash felt Del's hard gaze from beside her, but didn't turn to meet it. The last thing she wanted was relationship advice from the investigator.

Del said, "Well, that's probably between you and him."

"It's frustrating." Ash tried very hard not to raise her voice. "It makes him unwilling to listen to my ideas. It's the same thing with Karl and Olympia and everyone else in this damn colony. Why doesn't anyone want to hear what I say?"

"I'm not listening."

"Like, the other day, when I told Olympia that it would probably be perfectly safe to visit the other colony, she sarcastically said, 'Let's just walk over there and get it done with,' and I said, 'No, that would be stupid. It's too far to walk. Plus, you need to scrape the logs when you do it and back off if there are warnings.' She said that I was the stupid one, but I'm not. I know better than anyone how Traverse works."

"You're not the expert, Ash."

"I have years of education and experience. By definition I'm as good an expert as anyone ever gets."

"Karl has the same education as you and he's been scraping Traverse's logs for decades."

"So, Karl's a better expert because he's super old?"

"He's the same age as me."

"That doesn't mean he deserves my respect."

"It doesn't mean you deserve his," Del said, adding before Ash could respond with a clever retort. "Or mine."

The sun set, bathing the world in greens and yellows. Soon, three fat moons lit the rocky slope despite the clouds covering half of the sky, and the only reason they could spot the trail was the eight brilliant lights mounted to the front of Hector's spider. The slope leveled out, and the trail grew lighter. Ash climbed down to get a better look.

Del hit the ground next to her. "He must have passed this way after the storm completely stopped.

His footprints don't even show when he hops from rocks like these."

Even in the spider's bright lights, the trail became difficult to follow. Hector opened the front of his cabin and waved at Ash. "How's it going down there?"

"Just try to keep up," Ash said, sharper than she meant. She scrambled along the path, careful to check that they followed the footprints. It wasn't even footprints here. The occasional scuff mark or smear across the side of a stone marked evidence of the passage of life. An indentation in some saturated gravel. In a world devoid of any biological life of its own, this was evidence enough. Nobody traveled this far from Edge. She had to move fast, waiting only for the walker's lights to make their way closer to her. Hector's illumination was her only sight in the whole world, and all else was the blackness beyond.

"What were things like back then?" Ash asked. "When the colony was new?"

Del pointed to a mark in the mud that Ash had missed, and the two women moved forward. "It was tough. We did what we had to do."

"Wouldn't you have wanted help from another colony?"

Del's expression grew grim. "We don't have anything to offer the new colony."

"We have our experience. We could give them our records from those early years."

"Traverse does that already. That's exactly why it doesn't want us interfering directly."

"I just wish we could warn them about Traverse."

Del held up a hand, gesturing for Ash to stop. A slight drizzle had started and the path before them blurred.

Ash scoured the surrounding rocks. In the fierce spotlights of the big machine, color washed out of the landscape. Black turned to gray, and brown turned to a mixed grayish mud. There had to be evidence. He must have gone somewhere.

She remembered the old stories of Earth. Westerns, where men would track people through strange worlds covered in weird, pointy cacti. They would taste the soil and touch a broken blade of grass, making thoughtful noises. Then they would know where their quarry went. It was that easy.

Ash bent down. She touched the dried muck with one finger and dabbed it on her tongue. It tasted like bitter metal. She cocked her head and listened for as long as her short patience could possibly allow. Sound came to her in the distance, like the low hiss of an ancient snake, singing a song to its prey, warning of its coming.

But it wasn't a snake.

The first heavy raindrops fell like a plague of fat frogs slapping the earth. The trail would disappear in seconds if it even existed at all. It would wash away in the new layer of muck, gone forever.

"I've marked our location," said Del. "We can come back."

"No!" Ash stepped into the darkness beyond Hector's light. To her right, a long cliff dropped down into the darkness. Far below, the rocky shore ran along the edge of the thrashing ocean. Her eyes quickly adjusted to the fading moonlight. Only one moon lit up the night sky now, showing its silver face far to her right, where the clouds had not yet obscured the sky.

Upslope, then. Hand over hand, she made her way along the path, listening for movement ahead and peering into the deepest shadows she'd ever seen.

"Ash," said Del behind her. "Ash, come on, we're done here. We'll report this location and come back out in the morning."

The clouds covered the last moon. For several long seconds, the only sounds were the hissing of the rain and the *tap, tap, tap* of Hector's spider working its way forward up the slope.

Still, Ash couldn't bring herself to stop. She pulled herself up farther and farther, over the lip of a rise so that Hector's lights didn't blind her.

It was there she saw a light up ahead, bobbing as if enticing her ever forward. It glowed along the ragged rocks, dipping and dodging out of sight and back again. What was it? The yellowish glow grew closer.

Then disappeared.

Tap, tap, tap.

"Hector, stop!" Ash cried over the edge. "I saw something up ahead."

"What was it?" Del asked.

Hector dimmed his lights, then shut them entirely down.

Tap, tap, tap.

Ash felt Del's presence next to her but couldn't see her at all. She heard the older woman's breathing against the patter of filthy rain.

Tap, tap, tap.

"Hector, stop," Ash said, hoping he could hear.

"I stopped already," he said, his voice close.

Tap, tap, tap.

"Then what's that noise?" Ash asked.

The air shook with the howling scream of metal against stone. Light crested the rise of black rock, first eight yellow lights, then eight times eight. Times eight again. Blinded, Ash reached out, finding Del's arm.

Too many legs propelled a giant walker over the ridge. A multitude of arms bristled from its front. Black tentacles writhed in front of a wall of pure yellow light.

Then, it attacked.

CHAPTER FIVE

SHINING black tentacles swiped at Ash. Rocks clattered underfoot as she scrabbled back. A hundred points of light made shadows dance like menacing ghosts. How far back was the cliff? Would her next step plunge her into darkness below?

The tentacle machine lunged for Del, and Ash got a good look at it from the side. Its slick gray plating caught moonlight with an iridescent sheen. Hundreds of black arms bore wicked tools or piercing lights, all operating with uncanny independence. Del disappeared behind a granite slab, and the monster followed.

A shout stuck in the back of Ash's throat. Fear bubbled in her chest. If she shouted, it would come at her. If she ran, it would catch her. Fear froze her in inaction.

Hector climbed into his spider. Not that it would

do any good. The attacker stood twice as tall and wielded dozens of potential weapons.

Hector could give it a good wash if he was lucky enough to get close.

That brave idiot. He provided a distraction. If he could do it, then so could she, because he wasn't going to reach the spider in time.

"Hey!" Ash threw a rock at the spider.

A dozen lights turned in her direction.

"Yeah, that's right."

More lights turned toward her.

Damn.

Ash ran, jumping from slick rock to slick rock in the rising storm. She made her way along the top of the cliff. She could see the drop-off now through the smattering rain, gaping like a hungry maw to her right. If there were some way to send the monster down there, they could escape. Maybe she could lead it to unstable ground, but there wasn't any. Not that she could see within the halo of sun-bright glow surrounding the attacking machine.

Dark swallowed her whole as the monster's lights snapped away to focus the other direction. She teetered atop a boulder; fingernails bit deep into the blossom storm's muck. She lowered herself to the tight gap between crooked slabs of granite.

Somewhere in the night, metal struck metal, screeching like a cry of death. She had to get back there to help.

She had to get away.

Fear strangled her again and froze her in place.

Ash couldn't believe there could be a murderer, and now here they faced him down in this huge murder machine. They should have brought better weapons. Batons were a joke to that thing.

Not that anything she could have made would have stood up to that kraken.

Metallic screams echoed over the canyon, muffled by the hiss of the storm. Each drop of muck stung Ash's flesh with a cold slap. She cursed her stupid project and her audacity at releasing it on the world. What had she been thinking? The muck that fell from the sky tarnished this beautiful world.

Everything she did was a mistake.

Another thundering crash.

The monster's rays danced closer through the pouring rain. Through that reflection, Ash spotted her path forward up between the granite slabs. She swallowed fear and crept forward.

Lights shifted again, revealing a lone figure high on the ledge. In the brown-black shadows, the silhouette appeared deformed. Inhuman. As fast as the lights shone against him, they disappeared, but his image burned itself into the back of Ash's brain.

Shouts echoed from below. Then, another crash. The lights flashed over Ash once more.

"Run!" Hector shouted somewhere in the dark. "Ash, run!"

She stole one last look Hector's direction, and saw tentacles lifting Hector's spider above its head. It walked to the cliff's edge, its too-many legs finding purchase on the muck-covered rocks. Her heart slammed against the cage of her chest. How could he do this to her again?

Her panic tasted like acid and blood.

Then, the kraken threw. Black void swallowed the spider whole.

Rain intensified. She couldn't see more than a few feet in front of her, lit only by the far-off kraken's writhing lights. Ash couldn't move for the crushing fear.

Hector. Had he been in the spider when it fell? Could he have survived that?

Ash tried to force negative thoughts from her head, but they insisted. Burned. One step, then another. Upward, she moved. Her fingernails broke on granite as she pulled herself toward the place where the figure stood. She'd take him down, weapons or no. She'd fought monsters before.

She'd killed before, or close enough.

The thought stopped her for a split second. Is that really who she was? A person who kills killers? No, she *created* life in a lab. Assembled it, anyway. She *helped* people. Marta had been mentally ill. The woman hadn't deserved to die, no matter what horrors she had planned. Maybe it was the same for this monster.

Or maybe not.

She surged forward again. The lights dimmed as the black rain blotted out the world. The hiss grew to a roar. Her clothes hung heavy with muck. Thick with it. She heaved herself over one last slab to reach the summit.

The lights went black.

Several seconds passed and Ash stood perfectly still atop the ridge. The rain lessened; its furious assault eased. In seconds it became nothing but a light drizzle, as if nothing had ever roared from the sky.

A thread of silver moonlight glowed through the thinning clouds.

The tentacle monster was nowhere to be seen. Nor the figure. She tried to call out for Del and Hector, but her voice caught in her throat. What if they weren't there? What if the kraken killed them? Or took them? She shivered, either from cold or fear. This was her fault. All of it. She hadn't thought forward enough to understand that there would be danger. Not this kind of danger, anyway. Why hadn't she thought of that? What kind of idiot was she? Del was right. Ash was inexperienced and was never really an expert at anything. She deserved whatever she got, but Hector? Del? What had happened to them? What did they deserve for Ash's mistakes?

"Ash?" Hector's voice came from somewhere down below, and it sent a knife right into Ash's heart. He stood there, not twenty feet away, with Del next to him giving him support. "Are you, okay?"

Ash laughed despite herself. "Me? Am *I* okay?"

She ran down the rocks and slammed into him in a hug.

He let out an "Oof," but hugged her back.

Del said, "I'm sorry."

Ash pulled back. "What?"

"I knew if we found someone they might fight. I didn't know..." She held her baton at her side in a white-knuckled grip.

"You couldn't have known," Hector said. Something mournful rang through his voice.

"Your spider's gone, isn't it?" Ash said, squeezing his hand.

"I'm going to start to get a reputation if I keep breaking spiders."

Ash gave him a wan smile. "If anything, it's me who's going to start getting a reputation."

"Kid," Del said, "you've had a reputation for ages. It's those of us around you who should know better."

"We should get out of here," Hector said. "Before it comes back."

Ash led them through the maze of rocks. She knew the way to go, and without much trouble managed to get them back to the rocks where there had once been a trail to follow. From that direction all the rocks looked the same, but she knew the direction to town and the general path grew easier as they circled the long way around Edge.

After a short distance, Hector freed himself from Del and walked on his own. "Whoever drove that thing paused before tossing my spider over the cliff.

It's like they wanted to give me a chance to jump out."

"How kind," said Del.

Hector shrugged. "Maybe the driver just wanted to pause and decide whether or not to wreck such a good source of metal and parts."

"How do you think he managed to build a kraken?" Ash asked.

Hector shrugged. "Lots of engineers build strange stuff."

"You're calling it a kraken?" Del asked.

Ash said, "Nobody's built anything like that in our colony, right?"

"Not that I know of," said Hector.

"Kraken, though?" said Del. "That's a sea monster, right?"

"He must be from the other colony," Ash said, almost to herself.

Cold ached in Ash's bones as she walked through the night, but she kept placing one foot in front of the other. They'd failed, but they knew more than they had known when they set out. They knew the direction the killer had traveled outside of town. It should have been a relief, knowing that nobody in the lab had murdered Paige. It wasn't. The killer still walked free. And he had a kraken.

She didn't realize she had stopped until Hector put a warm arm around her. "We can take a break if you need," he said.

Ash shied away from him. "No," she said, her

brain numb from exhaustion. "We should get back. I need a hot shower and some coffee."

"Coffee sounds pretty good right now," said Del, apparently unfazed by the night's events. "I could go for a donut too."

Ash continued forward, this time with Hector right at her side. "We need to turn around right away and get back out there."

Hector said, "He'll be gone. He's had all night to clear out."

"He'll leave another trail."

"It was still raining when he left." He had the audacity to not sound convinced.

After a while, Hector said, "The walkers that the other colony built didn't look like that. It could be a custom build, but the way it moved was really strange. I don't even know how anyone would drive that thing."

The eastern sky glowed with the approaching sunrise, and Ash felt a second wind. "Then we really do need to turn around right away and get back out there. We'll bring a whole crew of spiders and something to take that thing down. We'll follow him all the way to the other colony if we have to."

"What about that shower?" Del asked.

"Well, yeah, we can take showers first."

"And some breakfast?"

"Look, I'm not a monster."

Hector said, "Good. Let's split up when we get to

town and meet back at the Commons. I might have something that'll help us against that kraken."

They passed the lava tubes just as the sun rose above the eastern rocks, expecting to find a mud-slick town gently rising from its slumber. Instead, they stepped into town to find a crowd gathering near the Commons. They made their way up the cobblestone streets, three muck-covered wanderers stepping out of the barren wastes.

Cynthia was the first to spot them as they approached. "I found them," she shouted back to the gathered group. She put her fists on her hips and narrowed her eyes. "Ash, is that you under all that mud?"

The crowd turned, and when Ash saw their wan expressions, she knew what had happened. "Oh no," she said, as the crowd parted. As she approached the scene, all the exhaustion of the night came tumbling back. They couldn't turn around and chase the killer out in the wastes.

Because the figure she saw couldn't have been the killer.

Lying before them was Morton Brooks, the janitor.

Dead.

CHAPTER SIX

"I THINK IT'S A SERIAL KILLER," Ash said, peering into her pint of nectar.

A thin layer of muck had covered Morton's body, so they knew he'd died around the time they'd fought the kraken. Del, tireless as she was, had sent Ash away with more samples to process.

After a quick stop in the lab, Ash had gone home to shower and nap in her little house, ignoring the steadily increasing tsunami of messages from Karl and Olympia. She could titrate another day. By the time she felt remotely human again, it was late afternoon, and she needed a drink.

Simon looked at her, his narrow face puckered with smugness. His gorgeous brown hair flopped to one side when he cocked his head. "Ash, there have only been two murders."

"Random murders. That's where the serial part comes in."

"What makes you think it's random?"

Ash threw her arms up in the air. "Why else would anyone kill Morton? He was the nicest guy!"

She must have spoken a little too loud, because the few other late-afternoon patrons at the Commons cantina cast some funny looks her direction.

Simon said, "Not everyone liked Paige and Morton, you know. It just happens that you like everyone."

"That's not true," Ash whispered. "I don't like Karl."

"Well, if he turns up dead, I guess we'll know who to interrogate."

Ash spun in her seat to scan the whole of the Commons. "He's not here, is he?"

"All I'm saying is that according to Olympia, people didn't really like Paige."

"Well, Olympia doesn't much like anyone, so maybe she's not the right person to ask." She narrowed her eyes. "Is she coming tonight?"

Simon drummed his fingers on the table. "She doesn't really come here anymore."

"She dumped you, didn't she?"

"It was the other way around, actually." A line formed between his bushy eyebrows. "She wants kids. You know, like Skye."

"You dumped her for that?"

"I'm obviously lying about dumping her, Ash. You're really a terrible investigator." He slumped.

"She cut me loose when she figured out how I felt. I realized suddenly that I was—"

"Severely outclassed?"

He smiled. "Yeah, pretty much."

Ash leaned over and clumsily slapped him on the back. "Hang in there, bud." She thought of Hector and the panic she felt every time they were close and how it slowly but surely was driving him away. "Relationships are the worst, and Olympia's a terrible person. She gave away my chocolate recipe to Cynthia."

"I thought Cynthia stole it."

Ash shadowboxed with her best impression of badass Olympia on her face. "Nobody steals from Olympia."

"True," said Simon, "but you're terrible with security, so she probably stole it from you. Anyway, I heard the recipe was a disaster."

Ash punched him in the arm, sloshing his drink onto his hand. "You heard that?"

Simon wiped up the mess. "I had Jasper in the Archives all day to record an interview. He brought Gerald and those two would not stop gossiping."

"Learn anything good for my investigation?"

"No, but I learned plenty about the life force." Simon swallowed the last dregs of his nectar. "Any progress with forensics?"

"That's confidential."

He waved his empty glass. "I'll buy you another drink."

Ash blinked slowly and peered down into her cup. The greenish liquid had somehow diminished itself until there was very little lingering at the bottom of the cup. This was a problem. "Deal."

Once Simon had procured new drinks for the both of them, he said, "I saw an old Earth show with a serial killer once. It ended up with a guy opening a box and there was a head in it."

"That's not how this is going to end up."

"Did you know that on Earth they used to kill people who killed people?"

Ash frowned. "We don't need to do everything earthlings did." Still, what would they do when they caught the murderer? Ash took a long pull of her nectar. "We'll figure that out when we get there."

"Hey, chances are we won't even figure out who it is."

"I don't understand why the scan is taking so long," Ash said. "In every Earth show I watched, it takes like two seconds to get a full DNA analysis, and our technology is way more advanced." She leaned forward and whispered, "Do you think Traverse is intentionally slowing things?"

"It's doing a lot more than simple DNA sequencing."

"Yeah. It is." Ash remembered that she wasn't supposed to have it do anything else. "Still, it doesn't seem like it should take so long. It's been over a day. When I added the samples from Morton, it looked like the Paige samples were still running, but when I checked the vials, they were completely empty.

"Empty?"

"Yeah. It's a destructive scan, so at some point they're going to be empty. But if they are, then why is it still running?"

"You know, I learned a little about this in school." He wiggled his fingers. "It's magic."

"No."

"Maybe you didn't say the magic words."

"Simon."

"Abracadabra. Hokey pokey."

"It's hocus pocus. There's a whole movie about it." Ash took a swig of nectar.

Hector appeared from absolutely nowhere. "I think you're thinking of hockey. It was a sport they played on ice."

Ash jumped up and threw her arms up in the air. He flinched, but that might have been because the alcohol in the nectar made her arms flail a little more than normal. "You made it!"

"Not much for me to do until the engineers finish the new rig."

"You could..." Ash chewed her lip as if she were thinking extremely hard about her suggestion. She pushed her nectar in front of him. "Have a drink. Simon's buying."

His face softened into a tired smile. "Don't mind if I do."

After Simon had grudgingly replaced Ash's lost

beverage, she said, "I think we should track down that guy, even if he didn't kill Morton. He might have still killed Paige."

"He almost killed all three of us," Hector said.

Simon leaned back and took a sip of his nectar.

"He didn't," Ash said. "I saw him up on the rise, you know." She closed her eyes and pictured him. "He had a huge head."

Hector frowned. "What?"

Ash gestured wildly to try to convey the strange shape of the person's shoulders and head. "It was dark, though. He was backlit, so I didn't really get a good look."

"Maybe it's some kind of mutant," Simon said.

Ash didn't think so, but it was a solid suggestion, so she let it stand.

Hector said, "If you saw him on the rise, then who was piloting the kraken?"

"Wait, a kraken?" Simon asked. "The sea monster?"

"It was on land," Ash said. "But yeah."

Simon took a long drink of nectar. "Damn."

"There might be two of them." Ash's head spun. Maybe more nectar would help. Nope. "No, I think the big-head one was controlling the kraken remotely."

Hector scratched his chin. "But why is he there at all?"

Simon said, "What if he's an outcast of some sort,

and he's coming to town to take resources little by little."

"You think he's a vampire?" Ash said.

"That's not what I said."

"Wow, a vampire. I'll need to do some research. They usually live in castles up on the hill, and they feed on the townspeople. Oh, and they're super sexy. Do you think he's sexy?"

"You said he had a giant head," Simon said.

Ash furrowed her brow. "Is that a yes?"

"Ash," said Hector.

She gestured, trying to convey the shape of the figure's body. "It was, like, a *really* big head."

Hector raised an eyebrow. "Can we get back to real murder-solving? We know your vampire didn't kill Morton."

Ash polished off the last of her nectar. "This isn't a work meeting, Hector."

"It is now," said a voice behind Ash. Del circled around to sit next to her across from Hector.

"Then we need more drinks," Ash said, waving for Simon to fetch another round.

"You know," Del said, watching Simon go. "If you had told me a week ago that there was going to be a murder, I'd have guessed it would be that boy murdering you."

Ash wasn't sure if she was supposed to laugh, but the nectar gave her sense of humor a little nudge, so she did. "He'd probably have to wait in line, because when I drink, I'm. Annoying. As. Hell."

Del thanked Simon when he delivered the drink. She took a sip and nodded appreciatively. "I just got back from the datacenter. All the screens are acting up, throwing glitches all over the place. I don't know if it's the excess rain or if there's something going wrong with Traverse, but it is impossible to do a deep delve into the video logs."

"I can do it," Ash said.

Del raised an eyebrow. "I brought you on to help with the forensic biology."

"Yeah, that's not going so hot."

Del closed her eyes and drew a long breath. "I shouldn't have brought you out last night. I'm sorry."

"No," Hector said. "I'm sorry. I should have picked up a different rig."

"No, *I'm* sorry," said Ash. "I froze when things started to go down. I was worthless."

"Both of you should have stayed in the colony," Del said. "It's not a matter of bringing the right rig. That outsider—"

"The vampire," Ash said.

"Wow, you are really annoying when you're drunk." Del paused long enough for even Ash to feel awkward. "The outsider couldn't have been our murderer. Not for the second murder, anyway. I still think there's someone in the colony killing people, and we're going to have to focus our efforts closer to home."

"Do you have suspects?" Simon asked.

Del paused to take a deep drink from her nectar. "You really want to be involved in this, Simon?"

"Not really, but I've bought enough drinks now that I don't think there's any choice."

"I think there's something in the video logs that Traverse keeps in the records. There's no video of the actual murder, but we should be able to see who was nearby."

Simon gestured to Ash. "Do you want to do the honors?"

Ash sat in a dull fog for several long seconds before noticing her cue. Then, with an exaggerated flourish, she drew the tablet from one of her enormous pockets. She'd won the glitch-free device from Simon and had since kept it almost perfectly safe.

"What is this?" Simon asked, aghast.

Ash put a thumb over the crack in the screen. "Nothing."

"It's cracked!"

"It was like that when I got it." It wasn't. She had dropped it once while trying to simultaneously search for a twenty-first-century sitcom and eat a peanut butter and banana sandwich. "Anyway, it doesn't affect how it works." She swiped the machine and a Traverse console opened. Navigating through menus, she found the entry for the morning's video logs.

"This is as far as I got," Del said. "But it took me an hour. Every menu option was glitched out, and it randomly navigated backwards whenever I looked at it funny."

Hector said, "She pretty much just uses it to watch old Earth media."

"I do not!" Ash gestured, knocking the tablet across the table. Simon caught it before it fell to the floor. "I use it for work too."

"Can you access the forensic results?" Del asked.

"Yes. That's why I brought it, but the scan isn't finished. All it tells me right now is that the rain muck is fifteen percent blue."

"Looks brown to me," said Simon.

Hector nodded his agreement.

Del frowned. "What can you find in the video archives?"

"It was supposed to be ninety-three percent blue, with some white mixed in. Instead it's a complex mix of colors."

"It's a turd storm," Simon said.

Ash absolutely destroyed him with an icy glare.

"Video archives," Del repeated in a voice that cut right through Ash's nectar haze.

Ash navigated through footage, forward through the hours of the morning until the approximate time of the murder of Morton Brooks. In another panel, she did the same with the morning of the Paige Liu murder. Both happened during a blossom storm, so every outside camera was a blurred haze of brown nothing.

But there were cameras indoors. She saw the

logged entry every time a person left their home or entered one of the nearby buildings. Reversing, she saw the entire morning's traffic, how people hurried along to get to their businesses before the storm hit, or how they saw the storm coming and refused to leave their homes. By the time she had a consolidated list of everyone out on both mornings, she'd sobered significantly. Unfortunately, a pointed look at Simon didn't earn her another drink.

Then, she saw the vampire. On the morning of Paige's murder, for a split second in front of the Commons building, there moved a man. He had long hair and a trimmed goatee. The hood of his black slicker dripped with the ebbing rain, but she had one clear shot at his face. He definitely wasn't anyone from the colony. He really was an outsider.

"The vampire," whispered Simon.

"But his head is normal-sized," said Hector.

"What?" asked the inspector.

"It's a long story," said Ash. "That's him. That's got to be our murderer."

Del said, "He wasn't at the second murder."

"Maybe that was a coincidence."

"Two murders in two days? That's not a coincidence, Ash."

"Maybe it was a *big* coincidence."

"You know, you're not drunk anymore, but you're still annoying." Del peered down at the screen sitting on the table before her. "There's more. Let me see your lists."

Ash brought up the lists.

Del took a moment to compare the lists. She spoke in a low voice. "You said that Leonard didn't have an alibi?"

"He said he was working on fireworks for the festival."

"Which would leave logs."

"That's right."

Del turned the tablet to face Ash. "And are these the kind of logs that would require a person to be present at his station?"

Ash peered at the screen, not comprehending at first. It was an activity log of Leonard's work through the times of both murders. He'd been working on a complex print of the components of some volatile ingredients—the kinds of things a person uses to make fireworks. It all checked out to her, except—

"He wouldn't need to be active during both windows." She highlighted the estimated times of the murders. During both, the printers were running but no user interaction was recorded. She remembered Leonard's scarred fingers. "I mean, for safety's sake he would have needed to be there, but Leonard's pretty sloppy for a chemist."

"He was always pretty careless."

Ash swiped through the logs. "I don't think it was him."

"You wrote down a *maybe* in your notes."

Ash tried desperately to drink the last drops out of her glass. "It's got to be the vampire." She swiped to the picture. "Look. This puts him right there, hardly fifty feet away around the time of the first murder."

Del said, "Ash."

"Why do people keep saying that as if it's going to stop me from what I'm doing?"

"I don't know," said Hector, shaking his head. "I really don't know."

"Dig into Leonard's background," Del said to Ash. "I'm going to bring him in and ask him a few questions. You figure out if he had any problems with Paige or Morton."

Ash looked to Hector for help, then Simon. Neither of them proved to be any good at all. "Fine," she said. "I'll ask around."

CHAPTER SEVEN

"Whatcha working on, Gerald?" Ash singsonged.

Gerald flinched. "Karl is looking for you."

"But he hasn't found me yet." She leaned over his shoulder and peered at his screen. Through a haze of glitches, she saw a schematic for a short, segmented worm. "Worms?"

He swept his black, unwashed hair to one side. "Worms, flies, spiders, birds, and then cats, maybe. I don't know. I'm working on designing the entire ecosystem, not just one little microbe like some people."

"It's a good microbe, though."

"I just wish the crap it created wasn't so damn complex that my worms can't process it." He smoothed out the annoyance in his voice. "What do you want, Ash?"

"You and Leonard came down from the ship in the same group, right?"

He sighed. "Yeah. It was years before you got here. Back when things were a lot quieter."

"Less glitchy," Ash said, looking at his screen.

"A lot less glitchy."

"Those were the good old days, huh?"

Gerald pulled up a chemical analysis of the segmented worm and ran a breakdown sequence showing its nutritional value to an insect. "They were."

"Makes a person pretty angry, doesn't it?"

He shot her a sideways look but didn't respond. On his screen, several red lines flashed, showing deficiencies in his simplified food chain.

"Morton was on your shuttle too, right? It's in the records. You don't have to answer."

"Lots of people were on that shuttle. Orson over at the Commons, Karl, couple people on the construction crew, and several janitors. Turns out sanitation is an essential function, and Traverse doesn't mess around."

"No, it doesn't, does it?"

On the screen, behind a haze of glitches, the segmented worm recalculated, giving it a different preconfigured digestive system. In the internal calculations, nutrients from the substrate processed through its system, balancing levels of various complex chemical interactions. "The life force of this planet must always be in motion to thrive, moving from one creature up the chain to another. Only then can the planet truly support itself and in turn support us." He ran his fingers through his hair and stepped back. "And you've started us off with the most complicated slurry of nutrients you could think of."

"It's not complicated," Ash said, looking at the screen. She was wrong, and she knew it. The precipitate was wildly complicated, with internal chemical and biological reactions burning through it, even after it landed on the ground. "It shouldn't be complicated."

"Well, maybe Karl's right that you ought to spend a little more time in testing. Your organism is mutating, consuming its own waste, and coming up with all kinds of strange combinations of chemicals. Designing something that can consume any one of those organic outputs without being poisoned by the others is an effort in futility."

Ash took a step back.

"If we can't figure this out, Ash, then you've killed us all and the planet along with it. We're all going to suffocate in your precrapitations."

"Blossom storms," Ash whispered.

"There's not going to be anyone around to call it that." He took off his glasses and rubbed the bridge of his nose. "Do you really think Leonard could have killed Paige?"

The question hung in the air between them while the flashing red of the display lit Gerald's pale face from below. His sad eyes in the dark shadows lent him a visage of madness, like he'd worked himself to exhaustion many times over without any thought of pause. She and her microbes had done this to him. Had she done the same to Leonard? To Olympia?

She said, "I don't think anyone could murder Paige."

"It is the nature of life to consume." He twitched. "If you don't believe murder can happen, then you're in the wrong business."

"It wasn't my first choice."

"But you weren't really good at your first choice, were you?"

Ash bristled. It was all she could do to remain polite with the older man. "The salicylic acid is poisoning your stupid worm. Add a gut microbiome to break that down, and it'll have the nutrients it needs to thrive and a significant boost in survivability, and also screw you very much." Well, she *almost* kept herself polite, and she deserved quite a bit of credit for that.

His face turned a deep red. "Leonard didn't kill her. If you haven't figured out that they were in love, then you're not particularly good at investigating either."

"They were in love? Both of them, or was Leonard in love with her?"

"They used to sneak off up to the reservoir at night to go for walks. You don't go for long walks like that if you're not interested in someone."

"I thought Paige was asexual."

"But not aromantic." Gerald stared at his screen as he talked. "She liked to be with people, she liked romance, but she didn't like sex. It's something Traverse selected for, actually."

Ash furrowed her brow, trying to puzzle it out. "Why?"

"People who like sex tend to have a higher percentage of unplanned pregnancies. That's inconvenient if you're an unfeeling, monstrous machine intelligence. People who don't form romantic relationships or at least close friendships tend to make trouble in small, close communities like new settlements. So, a romantically inclined asexual person like Paige is a good fit for a moderated colony."

"But not everyone can be like that." Could they? Could she? "Aren't you bisexual?"

"I'm not here to debate the techniques our robot overlord takes for managing population. You know better than anyone that what it does isn't always the best tactic or at all moral." He looked up from his screen. "And I'm pansexual."

If Leonard and Paige were together romantically, then that murder fit into an entirely different category. She had seen enough crime dramas to understand that most guilty persons were the significant others of the murder victim. The fact that they were together made Leonard look *more* guilty, not less. Even if he hadn't murdered Paige, could he have been guilty of murdering Paige's murderer?

Was Morton Paige's killer?

Even as the pieces fit together they fell apart. Ash couldn't imagine Morton or Leonard hurting anyone, let alone being guilty of murder. The relationship meant there were angles she needed to pursue, but it was all a distraction from what she really wanted to do: return to the vampire and figure out who he is.

"Thanks, Gerald," she said, "you've given me something to think about."

"Leonard didn't kill Paige," Gerald said.

Ash turned to leave, then made like she remembered one last thing. "Oh, by the way," she said, waiting for his full attention. "When you're doing your calculations, make sure you're taking into account the different nutritional requirements of people like Skye."

Gerald didn't move for a long time, not even to breathe. Ash thought that maybe he had frozen in place or he maybe was having some kind of absence seizure.

"Gerald, I—"

"Oh," he said. "Oh." He turned back to his screen and wouldn't respond to any more of Ash's queries.

It didn't matter. She had what she needed from him, and if the overworked man felt so energized about his work that he didn't want to talk with her, then that was just fine. Precrapitation wasn't even the best insulting name for her blossom storm, and he should really be ashamed of that.

On her way past, she swiped a piece of freshly printed weapons-grade chocolate and discovered that it really was a bitter horror worse than anything she had ever eaten. After ten minutes she was finally able to get the burnt socks flavor out of her mouth, but the memory would stick with her forever.

"Told you the recipe was bad," said Cynthia. "Too complex for our printers. It collapses in the third stage."

From there she visited Leonard's lab station—her old station. Dozens of biopacks cluttered the desk. The tightly packed bundles of chemicals might have been output from the printer or intended for input. Leonard's organization system made no sense, and Ash didn't look forward to digging through it. She ran a finger along the top of the screen and a spinning Traverse logo appeared. "Good times, lab. Good times."

This was where she had developed the scrubbers that actively cleaned the planet's air. They were thriving, which was great. At the time they'd taken over the incubator. Now they took over the planet.

She checked the logs to verify what she already knew of Leonard's activities. If he had been seeing Paige, he hadn't left anything about it in his journals, which Ash considered strange. Maybe she was the only one who made notes about potential lovers in her lab notes. Her titration logs were full of references to Hector's big arms that she desperately wanted to wrap herself around.

Nope. Asexual wasn't going to be her thing. Too

bad she had a panic attack every time she got close to the big man.

Ash wasn't sure what she was going to find at Leonard's station. Records fully admitting to the murder? A screed on the rights of biolab scientists to murder random colonists? She turned to the drawers and punched in the code for the top one. It slid open to reveal a jumbled mess of vials. When she lifted one up, it disturbed the whole mass and a lid fell to the floor and rolled under the desk.

She swore. Leonard was way less organized than she had ever been. Why didn't Karl give him a harder time about it? She got down on her knees and crawled under the desk. As her hand closed around the lid, she looked back to see two long legs with black curly leg hair poking out from under too-short gray scrubs.

Jasper.

The tall man muttered under his breath as he rummaged around Leonard's lab station. Ash pulled herself farther back under the desk, wondering what the biologist was doing raiding a fellow scientist's materials.

"Hah!" Jasper took a step back.

Ash peeked out from her hiding place to see Jasper pocketing a biopack and set off through the lab.

After a few deep breaths, Ash emerged from under the desk, watching as Jasper put on a big smile and approached Gerald's station.

Karl spoke behind her. "Miss Morgan."

Ash jumped. "I'll catch up on my work," she said, turning to him with her hands raised. This was all she needed. Karl would be his usual mean self, force her to stay and titrate some stupid liquids for Olympia, and then demote her again for all her efforts.

But what had Jasper taken?

Karl waved it off like it was nothing. "Don't worry about it, kid. You're doing important work and everyone appreciates it."

Jasper argued with Gerald down the hall, and Ash caught something about poison. She would need to follow up on that. Soon. "Do you know anything about Leonard?"

"He got his work done. Didn't cause any global crap storm. Little bit of a temper when he worked too hard." He paced as he talked, slowly circling around Ash like a wolf stalking its prey. "Looks like you might get your old station back."

Ash swallowed the lump in her throat. "Do you know anything about Leonard dating anyone?" She wasn't sure how much she should lead her interviewee, and the idea of interviewing Karl made her armpits sweat.

"What, he and Paige? They were friends. Maybe he wanted something more."

"You don't sound convinced."

"Are you asking if I believe Leonard is the murderer?" His smile was almost warm. "It's hard to believe it of anyone, isn't it?"

"Paige didn't murder herself."

Karl's expression grew hard again. "Thing is, you're under a lot of pressure. Life and death pressure."

"You think the murderer will kill again?"

He shook his head. "Have you noticed we don't have a prison?"

She had been trying not to think of that.

"Edge went through this early on. We can't have a murderer hanging around the colony, and we can't afford the extra expense of keeping him alive. If he's caught, he'll take his own life. That's the right thing to do for everyone, but it's still a death on your hands."

Ash tried to keep the quaver from her voice. "What if he doesn't?"

This time, his shark's grin was wicked as they come. "I'm sure you'll come up with a painless way to end it for him."

"We're not going to kill him."

Karl said, "No, I'm sure you won't have to. I know Leonard. He cares about this colony too much to make you go through all that." He sighed, and his shoulders slumped. "Once our colony crosses that line, there's no going back. It's not what any of us want."

Ash pressed her lips together, trying not to take Karl's bait. "I'll get back to work here soon as I can."

He smiled. "It's not a problem, kid. Work with Delilah until she doesn't need you anymore, and when you're finished you can have your old station back." With that, he disappeared back into his office.

A minute had passed before she remembered about Jasper. Both he and Gerald were gone, leaving Gerald's lab fully locked down. The biopack was nowhere to be seen. She searched the top of Leonard's desk, trying to remember what had been there before. What poison had Jasper taken?

Ash went back to Leonard's drawers, shaken by what Karl had said. If Leonard were the killer, would he really kill himself? She'd think about that when she found evidence, and Leonard wasn't stupid enough to leave anything in his lab drawers.

Except, in the bottom drawer, crammed way back behind her old backup recordings of Earth movies, she found a rock.

Only, it wasn't just any rock. It was a fist-sized chunk of glassy black obsidian with streaks of dark red running through it in a swirling pattern. Ash scrambled to find a specimen bag of the right size to pick it up. A sticky residue in its deep crevices held something that looked suspiciously like blood.

She had found the murder weapon.

CHAPTER EIGHT

Ash wore a crimson trench coat and matching fedora. Under that she wore a button-down white shirt and crisp suit pants, both cut with severe lines and an immaculate attention to style. With Traverse's help, she was even able to tie a black bowtie to complete the look.

Del had already interviewed their suspect, but she hadn't gotten enough. Ash came with evidence, accusations, and an attitude. There were very specific things she needed to know to finally break the case, and she knew exactly what she needed to do to make the man talk.

Almost exactly.

Mostly.

It was time to put some of her expertise to work and trust the instincts honed by thousands of hours of Earth media.

The makeshift jailhouse consisted of a large

interview room and a locked cell with a toilet and a bunk. The construction crew had thrown it up overnight and, at Ash's request, left all the usual tech connections out. Traverse wouldn't listen in on their conversations here if she could help it.

When she stepped into the interview room, she looked every part the dashing inspector. Leonard might not crack for Ash the scientist, but Ash the inspector? He didn't stand a chance.

She jabbed a finger at their suspect. "Why'd you do it, Leonard?"

"I didn't kill anyone, Ash." He drummed his scarred fingers on the fiber table. His shoulders slumped and even his explosion of gray hair sagged with exhaustion. "I told Del. I was working on fireworks when Paige was killed."

"Sure, sure." Ash took her tablet from her pocket and pretended to reference something there. "You were seeing each other, though?"

He found something fascinating about a tiny spot on the white table. His bent glasses slipped down on his nose, but he didn't seem to notice. "We were friends."

"Rumor is it was more than that. Maybe *you* wanted more than that and she didn't?"

"No, no, it's not like that." He let out a long sigh. "She didn't want sex, and that was an issue, but otherwise, things were going great." He looked up and met her gaze. "I can't believe I'm talking about this with you."

"Why's that?"

"Well, you and Hector..." He trailed off, but Ash waited a beat for him to continue. "I don't think you know what it's like."

"Sex?"

"Not having sex."

Ash tried to keep her face from matching her coat, but probably failed. Leonard assumed she and Hector were having a much better time of it than they really were. "I've been single before."

"That's not what I mean. I mean, you don't understand what it's like to be together with someone on a spiritual level, but not a physical one."

"How about if you just answer some questions for me."

"No." Leonard glanced at the door. "Del's already asked me all this. Aren't you supposed to be in charge of the forensic science?"

"It's taking a long time to finish. Do you know why that is?"

"Maybe because the scientist isn't doing her job?" Leonard snapped.

Ash poked at her screen. "The samples were tampered with. Someone got onto Olympia's lab station and sabotaged the scan."

"So, talk to Olympia."

"I think you took the convenient opportunity to mess with my tests."

"That can't be. Any scientist running a forensic scan would lock the entire rig."

Ash looked up. "You can do that?"

"It's in the manual."

"The what?"

Leonard sighed. "There's a manual. You're supposed to read it all the way through before you start working at your lab. It's full of safety protocols."

Ash watched his scarred fingers tap the table. Time to make some guesses. "Why were you upset with Paige that day?"

Leonard blinked rapidly, like she'd slapped those flimsy glasses right off his face. "She wanted to stop seeing me."

"Because of the sex thing."

"No. Well, sort of, but not how you think. She thought that she wasn't going to be adequate for my needs. I thought it would be fine. Love is the most important thing, you know?"

"Do you really think it's possible to have a relationship where one person wants sex and the other doesn't?"

"You and Hector? Really?"

"So, you would just wait around not getting any sex because you loved Paige? Forever?"

"You don't understand."

"I understand the concept that sexual frustration might build up over time and come out as an explosion of uncontrolled rage."

Leonard, for some reason, didn't see fit to respond.

"I'll have to give that some thought once I'm not so busy with this murder investigation."

He met her gaze again. This time, she saw the anger burning behind his eyes. "We were fine, Ash. Maybe not the picture perfect relationship you might read about in fairy tales, but we were fine. She would have come around."

"Or she wouldn't."

He held her gaze for several more seconds, then found that spot on the table again. "Or she wouldn't."

Ash let the silence linger for a long time. This time when she looked at her tablet to pretend to read something, she actually pulled up some information. "Do you know anything about a family of chemicals called batrachotoxins?"

Leonard twitched.

"That's what I thought. It's a toxin found on certain Earth creatures called frogs. Gerald has some frogs. A lot of them. They're cute little guys." She brought up a picture on her screen and showed it to him. "They excrete this toxin, which is extremely deadly in very small doses."

"I've heard of it."

"Thing is, there's no good reason to print any of this stuff." She paused, giving him a long time to sweat about it. "Do you know why I'm asking this, Leonard?"

He said, "Morton Brooks was killed with that poison."

"And do you know where I found logs indicating a print of that substance?"

"My lab station isn't locked."

"It was locked when I went to check the logs."

"Yeah, Ash. It was locked with the default passcode. Anyone who ever used that terminal could have accessed it, which is why you still knew the code for this investigation."

"It was really convenient. I couldn't get on Gerald's terminal at all."

"I bet."

Ash pretended to take some notes on her tablet. "Anyone?"

"Think about it. It's the default code and it's never changed. Anyone you told back when you owned it could have accessed it at any point."

"And who have you told? Did Paige know?"

"Are you saying Paige murdered Morton?"

"That seems unlikely," Ash said, chewing her lip. Her bowtie was too tight.

"Paige didn't kill him."

"It could have been her vengeful ghost."

Leonard's face turned red. "She was a kind person, Ash. You knew her. She'd never kill anyone. Not for anything."

Ash tapped her chin. "That's what I thought about you, Leonard, but the evidence keeps pointing your direction. What should I believe, the hard evidence or my instinct about what kind of person you are?"

"You have logs that could be doctored and a rock that could have been placed."

Both behind security, Ash thought. But maybe not if what he said about the passcodes was true. "You have motive. Nobody else has motive to kill Paige."

"Because I love her? If that's motive in your mind, there's something seriously wrong with you. Someone should tell Hector."

"Oh, he knows all about what's wrong with me."

Leonard leaned back and his chair creaked under his weight. "I can't help but notice that you had access to everything that got doctored. You didn't have any trouble going through everything at my station."

Well, she certainly hoped *that* didn't get mentioned in whatever trial they might have. She had an alibi, but, then again, so did a lot of people. She also hadn't been terribly secretive with her lab station's passcode over the years. That probably didn't need to come out either.

She leaned forward and whispered, "I want to help you, Leonard, but you need to give me something. Who else would have wanted to kill Paige?"

This question seemed to really give him pause. He blinked several times and stared off into the distance. "Nobody," he said. "You're right. There's nobody who would want to kill Paige." He swallowed. "We were supposed to meet that morning, but the storm rolled in so we didn't get a chance. That's really why I was in the lab. I mean, there were fireworks to make, but I was only doing that because Paige was late. It made me angry to be stood up like that."

"You thought she was stalling the hard conversation."

"Yeah. She was like that. She avoided confrontation whenever she could. I think I just hated the idea that the confrontation might be with me."

"You *hated* it."

He slumped. "It eats me up. The day before she was killed, she asked me whether it's better to confront someone directly with a disagreement or just pretend like it didn't exist."

"Pretend what didn't exist?"

"I don't know. I assumed she was building up courage to break it off with me." He studied his hands carefully. "I didn't kill her, Ash."

"Then why was the murder weapon in your drawer?"

"Why *would* it be? Don't you think I'd get rid of it?"

"I did an analysis of it, and it had traces of your skin cells." This was a lie, but what the hell. "How were you planning on destroying it? Wait until you had some time alone and run it through deconstruction?"

He blinked. "That would probably be the way to do it, but why wait? Why wouldn't I just toss it in the bulk recycler out back?"

"Witnesses, Leonard. Everybody can see that

recycler, and anyway, it's easy to see what's gone into it in a certain time period. Morton dumped some stuff in there the day of the first murder, but it was just a bunch of rocks, fiber stands, and a huge pile of vegetation. If it had been the fancy burgundy obsidian rock, we would have caught it right away. Your head's really not in the game here. Maybe that's why I keep finding evidence pointing to you."

"What else do you have?"

Ash set her tablet down on the table. "You had opportunity and motive, the murder weapon, and a reasonable expectation of walking free. Morton Brooks found the murder weapon while cleaning, so he started suspecting you. You did a quick print of a toxic molecule. It was easy for a guy like you, and it didn't take more than a few minutes. When the rain hit before he had a chance to tell anyone, you had plenty of time to print the tiny amount needed and touch him with it. It's a fast poison, and nowhere near as brutal as bludgeoning someone with a rock."

Leonard let out a long, shuddering breath. "I'm not a killer."

"We're all killers, Leonard."

Ash stowed her tablet in her pocket and made a show of getting up to leave. When she got to the door, she turned and said, "Oh, one more thing before I leave."

"Yeah?"

"Did I tell you Karl is giving me my station back?"

His expression didn't change. "That's great, Ash."

"But, maybe you can help me with this because I'll be designing experiments again. I'm going to try to make chocolate from a design I wrote while working for Olympia."

Leonard stared at her with a look of pure exhaustion.

"I'm just not used to printing complex organic molecules outside of the bit that prints living single pseudocell. I think it's a different subroutine, but I'm not really sure. Is it the same as printing solid chemical substances like with your fireworks?"

He blinked a few times. "The manual's pretty clear on this."

"But I don't like reading manuals."

"It says any time you make organic molecules you need to go into the organics submenu. Same as printing live pseudocells."

Ash winked at him. "Thank you, Leonard. You've been a big help here." With that, she left the interview room to find Del waiting in the next room, arms crossed and a decidedly unamused look on her face. Ash untied her stuffy bowtie and crammed it into a pocket of her coat.

"You've been watching old Earth shows again, haven't you?" Del said.

"Only a few episodes!"

"And you really consider that research for the case?"

"Leonard might not have done it. Does that help?"

"What makes you think that?"

"Batrachotoxin is really hard to print, a lot like producing some of the chemicals in chocolate. No way he printed it up fast. He would have used that as his defense if he'd known."

"He could have had a file configured for it already."

"True, but we wouldn't have been able to prove that unless we found the preconfigured datafile. We didn't, but he doesn't know that. He would have said 'No way I could have created it so fast, it's too complicated' but he didn't."

"It's true," said Leonard from the next room.

"I thought these walls were supposed to be soundproof," Ash said.

Del gestured for Ash to come close and whispered, "He's our only suspect right now."

"Also," Ash whispered, "when I asked if he knew how to print chocolate, he gave the wrong answer. Organic molecules don't go anywhere near the submenu where pseudocells are printed. It's an entirely different process, and if he had ever printed complex organic chemicals he'd know that."

"Are you saying we should let him go?"

"Yes," Leonard said.

"Shut up, Leonard," said Ash. "We should keep him locked up."

Leonard said, "What?"

Annoyed, Ash made her way out of the makeshift jailhouse, making sure Del followed. "I have an idea of who might know something."

"Who?"

"Our only real witness."

Outside, Hector sat in a brilliant red spider, its front legs geared out for heavy cutting and rock collection. It was as wicked a setup as Ash had ever seen, and it made her heart skip a beat just to see her big guy sitting in the cockpit. He looked fantastic kitted out in pilot gear.

He grinned. "It's the spider Marta brought from the other colony. I made them retrofit it with a copilot seat, upgrade the tools, and paint it red."

Ash's jaw dropped. She climbed up next to him and took her place. Copilot, indeed, it had the full setup, perfectly configured for a person twice her size. She didn't care at all. "Oh, Hector it's perfect!"

"Ash," Del said. "Who are you going to see?

Hector answered, "She wants to visit the guy."

"What guy?"

"He was there around the time of the first killing," Ash said. "We know he wasn't around for the second one, but he's definitely a witness for the first."

Del repeated herself, "What guy, Ash?"

"The outsider."

Del swore. "No."

"I can do this."

"You're here to run forensics."

"And interview witnesses." Ash flipped a switch

on the dash, which started to play a haunting tune—not at all what she expected. "The outsider is a witness."

Del ground her teeth. "You can't go out there again. Not even with this."

"What?" Ash asked, making a perfect impression of someone who couldn't hear Del's direct order. She pushed the button to close the clear cockpit cover. It slid quietly into place, and she giggled at the sleek beauty of it.

Outside, Del shouted and waved her fist, but Hector flipped a switch and the spider rose and walked away, leaving the woman in the dust.

Before she could think too hard about it, Ash leaned over, kissed Hector on the cheek, took his hand, and gestured for him to move the spider forward. Her heart rate quickened, verging on full panic, but maybe—maybe this time she didn't hate it?

She let go of Hector's hand and started messing with the dashboard. "This plays music, huh?"

A broad grin spread across the big man's face.

CHAPTER NINE

"Did you really need to stop by your house again?" Hector asked as Ash climbed back into the walker, "or was it just an excuse to pick up more music."

"We're going on a road trip, Hector. Tradition dictates that we need music."

"Does tradition dictate that we need roads?"

"No." Ash uploaded a playlist to the spider's internal audio system and selected the first song. "This is a list of music that's all about cars and roads. It's all we need."

They left town through the quarry. As they crossed the open field, Hector said, "This is a decent tune, but what the hell is a lowrider?"

"I think it's a kind of car designed for really flat roads."

"Weren't their roads always flat?"

"Lowriders ride low to the ground in order to

improve aerodynamic efficiency. Their drivers were extremely concerned about carbon dioxide emissions from combustion engines."

"Huh."

"So, this is the reservoir?" Ash said as Hector's spider carried them past a stocky storage building at the top of the quarry. Three squat, cargo-hauling spiders stood next to the small building. A vast lake spread out behind the shed, its murky waters dark as a killer's soul. "I don't think I've been up here."

"A lot of us avoid this place if we can," said Hector. "It's generally off limits, except when people come here to drop something in long term storage. It's the most direct route to the location where we were attacked."

"By the kraken."

"Yeah. By the kraken."

The reservoir wasn't the colony's only source of water, but it played a large part in Edge's long-term viability. People could survive on surprisingly little water if they had proper recycling, but being able to use the reservoir helped significantly for anyone not really interested in drinking their own urine.

"You've been up here lately?" Ash peered into the still water. Its surface appeared clear, but the muddy rain still clouded the deeps. As they rounded the lake, the reflection of the low sun set the whole thing alight with blue fire. This was where Leonard and Paige spent their evenings together. "It's beautiful."

"They sent crews up here to rebuild the filtration system." Hector said, a hint of annoyance in his voice. "But I wasn't on them."

The implication hung heavy in the little cabin for a long while. Ash knew why he hadn't been able to help with the refit of the filter system. It was because he'd gotten street cleaning duty after wrecking his spider, which had been Ash's fault. The very fact that the streets needed cleaning was also Ash's fault, along with the need for advanced filtration. Maybe *everything* was Ash's fault in one way or another.

The walker moved along the lakeside path, picking its way up the tumbled rocks as easily as if it were moving through cobblestone streets.

"This is a smooth ride," Ash said. "It's nice."

"Yeah."

"Who'd you need to bribe to get it?"

Hector concentrated very hard on his driving for a while. Finally, he said, "I signed up for the deconstruction crew."

"Deconstruction? But I thought—"

"I like it better than cleaning, and there isn't as much construction happening these days."

Ash said. "The only thing being built is that filtration system, so I guess the crews can thank me for that." She meant it as self-deprecating humor, but it sounded to her ears like a cry for pity.

All Hector said was, "Yeah."

The sun set below the horizon, and Ash's palms went sweaty with the thought of being stuck out in the barren land at night. To her relief, Hector flipped on the night vision view of the landscape, complete with a display of their intended direction and a glowing light to lead them back home. The display grounded and comforted her, and she gave Hector's big arm a hug. Her heart raced at the touch, but it wasn't so bad.

The soundtrack rolled on with a song about a little red corvette. Ash understood why it landed on the road trip list. It was fun and groovy and had the kind of energy a person needed to pay attention for a long drive.

"I don't think this song is about a car," Hector said.

"That's ridiculous. This song was written by a prince of America in the twentieth century. They were *really* into cars during those days."

"I thought America was a democracy."

Ash frowned. She loved ancient Earth media, but politics were not really her thing.

Hector mercifully changed the subject back. "This spider is designed for exploration," Hector said. "I've been working on it for the past couple months, but now I've finally convinced them to let me activate it."

"It's wonderful." Ash looked at the other labels on the display. "Is that a defense system?"

"Blades and a cutting torch," he said. "In case we run into trouble again."

"Weapons?"

An uncharacteristically wicked grin flashed across Hector's face. "If we need them."

"But just for defense, right?"

Hector was silent for a beat too long. "Yeah."

Ash had a sobering thought. "Building weapons feels like preparing for a war."

"War might be coming for us whether we prepare or not," Hector said.

"How did you get Traverse to allow weapons?"

"They're not exactly weapons."

"And I don't exactly like it."

Hector grunted. "We're here to talk, but that doesn't mean we don't need to defend ourselves."

"Hector."

"We're doing something dangerous, Ash." His voice came out as a low growl, but it might as well have been a shout. "You always barrel ahead without any thought about consequences, but this is terrifying." He gestured at the land ahead of them. "We *know* there's someone hostile out there, even if it's not our murderer. We also know that the land itself is dangerous, and there's another colony full of people who might just react violently if we surprise them. What are you even thinking right now that you're not terrified of all this?"

"It'll work out."

Now he really shouted. "Because it always does, doesn't it? Even when it rains crap from the sky you're telling us it's going to work out. Open your eyes, Ash. It's not working out."

Ash pulled away from Hector and shrank back into her seat. Her heart raced like she'd just sprinted a mile. "Then we adapt."

"Adapt? Like how Skye is adapted? Ash, that's next generation. We'll be dead before we adapt like that."

There was a way. Wasn't there a way? Ash's brain raced, unable to come up with the right answer —the solution to all the doomsaying Hector spouted. How could he be so negative? How could he make her feel like this. She was—

Scared.

Ash didn't like feeling scared.

She remembered the terrifying storm that had killed Marta and the shadow of fear she felt every time she tried to get close to Hector. "I was getting better," she said. She *had* been, but now that was worse. Her heart wouldn't stop racing. Her fists wouldn't unclench.

Hector said, in a calm voice, "I'm tired of this."

"Tired of what? Tired of me? You're driving me all the way out here to break up with me?"

"Are we even together?"

Words stuck on Ash's tongue. They were caustic and vile, and Ash didn't like them one bit. "I thought we were," she whispered instead.

"You can barely touch me. You're not happy,

Ash. Every day is a struggle, and you won't let me help. Or Simon or Olympia."

"Olympia has issues of her own, and she keeps making me titrate liquids. Do you know how much better the automated systems can do that? It's not even close! They have me doing busywork because they can't handle that I'm so much more advanced than any of them in the art of creating elegant micro-biological solutions."

"Check your ego, Ash," he said as the spider mounted a particularly large boulder. "Popular consensus isn't exactly on the side of your blossom storms."

On the radio, a musician started singing about being taken down to paradise city in screeching high-energy lyrics that made Ash's teeth hurt. She mashed the stop button, and when that didn't work, she mashed it harder.

The third time she tried it, Hector grabbed her wrist. "You have to press the other button," he said, nodding to a blue button with the stop symbol on it. "This one isn't for the music."

"It says stop."

"I know, but it's not stopping the music, is it?" His tone was as condescending as it could possibly be.

Ash pressed the other stop button, and the music ended. She managed to say "Thanks," with an absolutely heroic effort.

They rode in an oppressive, eternal silence. Outside, the rocky terrain rolled by, rough stone towering tall above Hector's monstrous spider. They would have struggled to walk this way, and she understood why the vampire might visit their colony via the longer route. Still, this was the faster route, and the man could have ridden in his strange kraken. Couldn't he?

Why didn't he?

She remembered the silhouette she'd seen on the rise. It had been a person, but with that odd shape, she didn't know what she could expect when they went to visit him. Even if they surprised him and kept him away from his kraken, there was someone else there. Someone terrifying.

Ash stewed alone in her thoughts, unable to share with Hector and unable to drown the ideas in music. She pushed the forward button again and played the next song.

"Mustang Sally," she said. "I've heard this one before, and it's good."

After a while, Hector said, "I'm not sure this one is about cars either."

Ash frowned, considering the lyrics. "It is. A mustang is a kind of car."

"I thought it was a horse." One of the things Ash liked about Hector was that he really did know a lot about Earth history.

"They were *really* into cars," Ash said. "They named their horses after cars."

"Are you sure it's not the other way around?"

Ash chewed her lip. "Do you think we could have horses here on Sky someday? Maybe not regular horses, but an adapted equivalent?"

Hector concentrated on his driving for several minutes. "That's not really my area of expertise."

"No, but do you think we *would*?"

"You folk seem really concerned about what function things have. Would one of those huge, long-legged beasts have any real function if we have machines to do the heavy work and there isn't anything around that eats them."

"We'll have a microbiome that'll consume anything, even horse."

"Yeah, that's comforting."

"That's how it worked on Earth. Even the biggest creatures were part of the cycle." Ash felt herself move to the edge of her seat, which was pretty common whenever she talked about microbiology. She hadn't exactly forgotten about Hector's offenses, but all that was a vague buzz in the back of her brain. "There's bacteria and fungi that break down every-thing. They used to bury people in the soil to make it happen faster, but then they packed their bodies full of poison so it would happen slower."

"That's really weird."

"I know, right?"

Hector blew some air out between tight lips, like he was trying to keep himself from engaging in a fascinating conversation. "Didn't these bacteria and fungi attack living people?"

"Oh yeah, all the time. Lots of them were really dangerous."

"And you're replicating that?"

Ash thought of Gerald's food chain and how he likened it to life force moving from the tiny creatures up to larger ones. "We're designing our own systems to be safe for us. Or at least controllable."

Hector looked up at the sky. "Can you really control it once it's in the wild?"

"Not really."

They rode in silence again. Ash fidgeted, suffocating under the long, awkward tension between them. She listened to a string of songs from the late twenty-first century, marveling at the influences of their thumping rhythms and clean guitars. They were clear derivatives of music from the earlier age, and when she listened closely she understood what Hector had been telling her.

"It's all about sex!" she said.

Hector let out a surprised snort of a laugh.

"What?"

"Nothing," he said.

"No, really. What's so funny?"

"I didn't think you knew about sex." He smiled as if he thought it was a joke.

"I've had sex, Hector." Her palms went clammy and her heart started racing. Panic pressed at the inside of her chest. "Good sex, even."

"Just not with me."

Ash seethed. She wanted to snap back with something really clever, but nothing came.

Hector pointed forward at the amber vision of the night terrain. "We're here."

Ash leapt out of the spider before it had fully stopped. Before them stood a structure of stone, looming and squat against the night sky. Its gate looked to have been hewn from the mountain itself, made to look carved and ancient by whatever process had manufactured it. Near the structure sat the oily black lump of the mechanized kraken.

"Well?" Ash called back to Hector. "Are you going to destroy the kraken with your fancy weaponized spider?"

"I'm not here to start a fight," Hector snapped. "Remember?"

Hector powered up some dim headlights, and the rock face lit up in an array of black reflections. Obsidian. Ash rubbed several sections of it clean, finding large deposits of the glassy black rock. The light also revealed pitting and scarring across the front of the gate. She made her way across the broken earth to the door. Swallowing her fear, she picked up a rock and pounded it as hard as she could three resounding times.

"Hello!" she said. "We're here to talk!"

For a long time nothing moved. The black of night closed in around them, entombing them in the vast void. It was profoundly isolating—crushing, even —but Ash shrugged it off. She had Hector watching her back, and it didn't matter that he was strong and powerful and capable of crushing that stupid kraken with his dangerous new spider. What mattered was that he was a good man.

She thought of the little red corvette. He was pretty sexy too. Maybe she'd have to tell him that.

Then, the door opened to reveal a strange and gorgeous man like none she had ever seen.

CHAPTER TEN

WITH A SHARP JAWLINE and eyes of the deepest night, the beautiful man stood taller than anyone Ash knew in Edge. He wore a cape with a red and black collar that stretched higher than the top of his wildly luxurious glossy black hair. Embedded in that hair were rows of golden thread that fell braided upon his shoulders. Some strands of gold connected directly with a row of elegant tech circling the base of his collar.

"Antenna," Ash whispered to herself.

He cocked his head, fixing her with his penetrating gaze. "Excuse me?"

"You don't have a gigantic head." She gestured, indicating all of him. "Your silhouette looked strange because of your—outfit."

To her right, the kraken twitched as if waking from a sleep. Behind her, Hector's spider crouched, ready to pounce.

Ash raised her hands high, palms forward so he would know she was unarmed. Mostly. Her baton still hung at her hip, but who was going to be afraid of that? "I'm here to talk."

The man studied her for several seconds, then peered at Hector in his spider.

"He'll wait here," Ash said, trying not to imagine the frown of his disapproval.

"I have been expecting you," the man crooned. He disappeared back through the door.

Ash was not surprised when the door closed behind her. She swallowed back her apprehension. Everything would work out. It would be fine.

Dim light illuminated columns of rough-hewn stone propping up a heavy gray ceiling. On the opposite wall stood another enormous door, slightly ajar. The man hung his cape on a nearby hook. Without it, his tall form sunk into deep shadows. The golden weave remained in his hair, but he loosed the braids to let it drape across his back.

"It has been a long time since I have had visitors," he said, his accent thick and sharp.

"You're a little out of the way."

The man crossed to the opposite door and placed a hand on it. Without turning back to her, he said, "I am called Victor Lazal."

"Ash Morgan," Ash said.

Victor pulled the door open and passed through into blackness. From inside, he said, "Come, share a meal with me."

Ash thought about where his food must have come from. It was stolen from the colony. Was it really right to depend on his resources? Then again, anything she ate would be returned to the colony. Was it right to *not* eat as much of his food as possible?

"There is nothing to fear," he said. "The food is safe."

Did he think she hesitated because she thought he would poison her? "I have some questions for you about your recent visit to Edge."

"Edge?"

Ash passed into the darkened room, finding that it did have its own dim source of light above a grand table. "Our colony is called Edge because it sits on the edge of the mountain overlooking the ocean."

"This describes many places."

"Sure, but this one is ours, and we call it Edge."

Victor gestured to a chair at the table and seated himself directly across. "We have much in common, Ash Morgan. Those around us may not appreciate our brilliance."

Ash seated herself. The chair, like everything else in the vampire's home, was carved from a solid lump of stone. It was surprisingly comfortable, but the table and chairs were built to the large man's proportions, so Ash felt like a child. "Nobody appreciates microbiology."

"I was an engineer in my colony," he said. "And I specialized in creating tools to help form this planet and its people."

"That antenna was your invention?" she asked, gesturing at the golden weave in his hair.

"The neurological link is mine. The cape was someone else's affectation. The high collar dampens outside electrical interference on my neurological receptors." He touched his brow, where the golden weave sunk deep into his skull. "Alone this gives me rudimentary control over my Land Octopus. If I need to do detail work, I must wear the cape."

Several insectile machines the size of hands scurried across the ceiling, bringing plates and utensils.

"We call it a kraken," Ash said.

"Excuse me?"

"You know why we came here," Ash said. The food in front of her smelled wonderful. Somewhere in his keep, Victor must have had a good food printer. The steak in front of her dripped with juices and filled the room with its rich aroma. Everything had a strange smell to it, but she attributed it to a difference in the spice configurations. The insect deposited a sharp knife next to her plate and then filled a glass with a thin red liquid that smelled of alcohol and fruit. She took a sip. It was dry and tart, like no nectar she had ever tasted. "I want to know what you saw that morning."

"The activities of your colony are no business of mine."

Ash carved a corner off the meat and took a bite. It melted in her mouth. "How often do you visit our colony?"

"Often enough."

"You take our food, slowly draining the lifeblood from our struggling people. As far as I'm concerned, you may as well be a resident of Edge."

He spread his palms. "And yet, I am not."

"I know you were there at the time of the murder. You were raiding our recycler during the storm so that Traverse wouldn't see you on any cameras. You got caught, though. There were images of you moving through town."

"But no evidence of me stealing." His accent grew sharp as the knife in his hand.

"What did you see that morning?"

Victor took a bite. He chewed it for what felt like forever, but Ash forced herself to be patient. When he spoke, his voice was so quiet she could hardly hear. "Not all is what you think, and the god above will only allow so much truth."

"I think you witnessed a murder."

For a second, his eyes went dark, but he straightened, and the expression disappeared. The insect returned with a basket of fist-sized rolls. "They have never quite managed to properly make bread in a food printer, do you know that? They can't even make decent bread using a printed flour substitute. It has to be grown. The yeasts, cultivated."

"Some things are harder to make than others. We recently tried to make good chocolate."

He scoffed. "Impossible. The technology for molecular printing is not so precise as that."

"There are some quantum effects," Ash said. "Even our best pseudocell printers have a terrible failure rate."

Victor took a bite of his bread and said nothing as he savored the morsel.

Ash scowled at her plate. She picked up the roll and gave it a sniff. It smelled of warm yeast with a gentle hint of salt. She took a small bite and was rewarded with a salty crust and the most wonderful combination of flavor and texture she had ever experienced.

"It's the yeast, you see," said Victor. "And the glutenous structures in soil-grown wheat. Of course, it is not efficient growing and producing these ingredients. Not with the planet in its current state. For me, though, such things are simple. I've printed the seedstock from records and, as you know, the single-celled organisms were trivial for our baseline technology."

Ash spoke around another bite. "I wouldn't exactly call it trivial."

"No, that I'll grant you." Victor smiled. "But bread yeasts are an interesting thing. It is important to introduce a monoculture to your dough. That becomes the strain of yeast that dominates the process, turning sugars into alcohol and gasses." He raised his glass and took a sip. "Much like the fermentation of alcohol. The real flavor of bread comes from the mixture of other microorganisms. Those come from a thriving environment and from the very hands of the baker. Over time, they may mingle with the original strain, making a sour dough that can be propagated down the line for generations." Victor met her gaze with a grim expression. "But the original strain must be given time to find its strength. Introduce too much too early, and the whole thing is ruined."

"It's good bread," Ash said.

"Managed properly, a mix of organisms working toward the same goal may come up with a wildly different result that is at the same time quite similar. Managed poorly, the product is spoiled."

The last bite of bread stuck in Ash's throat and she couldn't respond.

"Edge is in trouble, Ash Morgan," said Victor. "You are the original strain, pure as the monoculture of yeast. You can continue this way, but not indefinitely. Your Traverse knows this, as does the instance of Traverse at the nearby colony."

"What does that make you?"

"I am here to ensure you never meet."

"Because Traverse would kill us all?"

He used his knife to carve another piece of meat. "The murderer you seek was not from the other colony. This, I can guarantee."

"How do you know?" When he didn't answer, she asked, "What can you tell me about the killer?"

Victor shrugged. "Fear is a powerful emotion, Ash Morgan. We never know how individuals will react when placed in the crucible of fear."

"Thanks, Victor. That's really helpful," Ash deadpanned.

The man ignored her sarcasm. "I wasn't in Edge to steal food."

"What did you steal?"

"There is a scientist attempting to bring higher scale lifeforms to the planet."

"That's Gerald. He's made worms, insects, and frogs, but they're not very viable as an ecosystem."

"And there is another man—a chemist. They were both in the lab when I looked in. Whatever happened in the front did not involve those two men —not directly, anyway."

Ash stood. "You're saying it was someone else?"

"I saw those two. I heard a shout over the downpour, and I saw that they were not involved." When Victor stood, it was like the unfolding of an ornate knife. He kept going and going until he towered above Ash. "That is all I know of your murder."

"Who then? It wasn't Olympia. If you say it was Olympia I'm going to punch you."

"By the time I rounded the building to help, there was only a body in the last fall of rain." His pale face betrayed no emotion. "So, I left."

"You're saying you can't tell me anything useful?"

"I can only tell you what I know," he said. The golden weave in his hair brightened, and three insects came through their passages to clear dishes. "Now you will be on your way."

"I do not think so." Ash unclipped the baton from

her belt. "You need to come back so that Del can question you."

Victor's expression darkened. "I will do no such thing. Be gone, Ash Morgan."

Ash took a step forward. "I don't think so."

An insect lunged at her. On instinct, she raised an arm to fend it off. Its pincers clacked inches from her face. It fell to the floor and cracked in half.

When she looked back, Victor was gone, but she caught the last movement of a panel in the wall.

"Oh no you don't," she said. She clawed at the heavy stone, but couldn't open it. Her heart pounded at the failure but she kept clawing. Until she found the catch. The heavy section of wall swung for her, opening to a long dark hall.

The maze swallowed her, and her eyes adjusted to the dim orange light. It flickered like flame, but her eyes couldn't focus on the source. She passed black, open doorways, but she pressed forward, listening carefully for any hint of the man's movements. When the hallway branched, she picked left at random. Then at the next branch chose right. Soon, she was lost.

"You need to come back for questioning," she yelled. "It's not like I think you killed him, but you might know something we need."

A scuff of a heel sounded from Ash's right, so she ducked down that corridor as fast as she could. The tail of a shadow disappeared around a corner.

Her grip tightened on the baton.

"I'll have Hector tear this place apart looking for you," she said. "We need to know who killed Paige and Morton."

The passage opened to a large circular room. Above, the ceiling disappeared into the inky black. Rows of boxes formed a circular pattern in the room, each filled with rich black soil. Many of them teemed with plants, from tall, yellow grasses to vines that spilled across the walkway. The air hung heavy with a thick humidity. Tendrils of green vines dangled from above. They were grapes, Ash thought. Or something nearly like it. She stopped and listened.

The swish of rough cloth. Up ahead. Ash pushed forward into the vast room until she saw the spiral staircase at its center. She walked to its base. Above, she felt movement in the air, and she took the stairs two at a time until it opened to a vast sky filled with moons and stars.

They were on a tower, and Victor stood silhouetted by the bright moonlight. He wore his cape, and the collar stretched up high above his head. In his silhouette she saw the same twisted figure the night they first met the kraken.

"You have real soil," she said. "And you grow real plants."

"Soil from my home," said Victor, "is my most valuable possession. Now be gone or I will destroy your friend."

Far below, a crash thundered in the night. Ash rushed to the railing and saw Hector's spider clashing with Victor's many-tentacled kraken. Again and again, they smashed together, the cutting torch Hector wielded making short work of individual tentacles, but there were so many. Too many. A flash of fire lit up the night.

Panic boiled in her chest. "Call it off," Ash said.

"You were my guest, Ash Morgan, and it was pleasant to speak with you." He backed away from her.

"Leave him alone or he'll destroy your Land Octopus." The quaver in her voice no doubt ruined her bluff.

"I was given a choice by our god above. I could conform and be one of the many or I could be myself out here in the vast nothing. I chose this life, and this is where I will stay."

"You visited Edge."

"I bring no harm to your people."

Ash's heart slammed against her ribs. "You're hurting us now."

Victor's lips pressed into a line. "Who is the intruder here, my dear?" A hint of fear showed in the corners of his eyes.

Below them, the machines clashed again, and Hector's spider heaved the tentacled monster into a wall hard enough to shake the rock under Ash's feet. The monster hardly slowed.

"We'll leave!" Ash shouted. She couldn't let them fight. The thought of losing Hector sent a red-hot poker through her chest. "Just call it off!"

Victor stepped up onto the stone railing. Below, the kraken broke from the spider, and silence filled the night from one horizon to the next. "If you are wise, you'll not contact the other colony. It is forbidden, and I will stop you if you try."

With that, he turned, spread his arms wide, and stepped backward off the ledge. Ash rushed across the tower to look over the edge, but when she got there all she could see was the black shadow of the rocks below.

Then, far away, she saw a slight flutter of black, like a bat flying through the night. It landed atop a moonlit rock and for a moment his form stood perfectly still, bathed in the silver glow of starlight.

"Damn," Ash whispered to herself. "He really is a vampire."

CHAPTER ELEVEN

"I TOLD YOU, HE CAN FLY," Ash said, finishing the long description of the previous night's adventure. Ash, Hector, and Del entered the jailhouse after a long conversation during breakfast at the Commons, during which they went through the entire experience several times.

Del adjusted her glasses and peered down at the papers on the table in the center of the room. They had written out details on their main suspects: Leonard and Victor.

"That explains Gerald's statement about the outsider moving downslope so fast after Paige's murder," said Del. "You think this Victor is innocent?"

"Absolutely," Ash said at the same time Hector said, "No."

Ash kicked him under the table.

"What?" Hector said. "His kraken attacked with

no warning at all. I could have taken it, but it was ugly."

"He used the attack to distract me," Ash said.

"Well, that wasn't much of a challenge, was it?" Hector flinched as if he knew his words were too harsh.

Del sighed. "Kraken."

"Victor called it a Land Octopus, but that's way worse."

"So, you and Victor had a good chat about it?" Del asked.

"I was his guest, and he invited me in for dinner," Ash said. "He told me he saw Leonard and Gerald in the lab at the time of the murder."

"See?" said Leonard from the other room. "I'm innocent!"

"Shut up, Leonard," Ash said. "He's probably right, though. I think this exonerates him."

Del shook her head. "A witness we can't trust or interview properly isn't really good enough to exonerate anyone."

Ash said, "You're talking about killing the murderer without irrefutable proof."

"Worry about the truth, Ash," Del said.

"Not the consequences," Ash finished the thought through gritted teeth.

"Shouldn't be a problem," Hector muttered.

Ash clenched her fists under the table, keeping her focus on Del. "You're just going to keep pushing, even though you know Leonard's innocent?"

"We don't know that."

"*I* know it. Isn't that good enough?"

Del spoke through gritted teeth. "You're not the only one who's been busy."

Hector said, "What do you have?"

The investigator pushed her papers across the table so Ash could read the data printouts. "Remember that poison that killed Morton? I thought I'd do a broad search through the logs for similar substances. Organic compounds of known poisons. Turns out there are a few of them."

Ash blinked. "Oh! Poison. I forgot about Jasper."

"What about him?"

"He picked something up from Leonard's desk while I was there. I think he and Gerald were arguing about poison."

Del stared at Ash forever before saying, "I didn't see this in your notes."

"I looked through the logs," Ash said. "There wasn't any poison."

"Look closer." Del jabbed her finger at the printout. "There are experimental variations on that batrachotoxin. Ways to suspend it in water. Ways to deliver it into the bloodstream via touch or ingestion. Deadly stuff. Weaponized versions of something already dangerous."

Ash stared at the printout. There was no way she could have missed the obvious experimental simulations. Or was there? Ash turned the paper so she could read more easily. "Leonard's been printing a lot of it."

Hector said, "Should I go get Jasper and Gerald?"

"Might as well just round up everyone," Del said.

When Hector moved to leave, Ash said, "Not yet, Hector."

Del said, "There's enough poison here to kill everyone in the colony. Twice. You could wreck the water table for a generation with a payload like this."

Ash called out, "Nice work, Leonard. Embedding it in a cubic white phosphorus crystal. Brilliant. Is that the poison Jasper took from your station? Is he in on it too?"

"I don't know what you're talking about," Leonard said from behind the door.

Hector leaned forward. "Is there another use for something like this?"

"No," Ash said. "There really isn't. Hey Leonard?"

Leonard said, "I'm supposed to be quiet."

"Who else has been using your lab station?"

"My printer has been making fireworks nonstop."

Ash rubbed her temples. Was he making fireworks or poison? If it was poison, what did he need so much for?

"Do you have what we talked about in the lab?" Del asked Ash.

It took Ash several seconds to understand the question. "The equipment's ready and the material is primed." Ash glanced at the clock. Traverse would be below the horizon for another hour. If they wanted to run experiments without the AI's explicit interference, now was the time. "Let's go."

"You're leaving me here?" Leonard asked through the door.

"We'll be right back," Ash called out.

The three crossed the colony to the biolab where Ash had taken over Leonard's lab station. The place felt abandoned, with only a few scientists toiling away in their respective stations. Jasper and Gerald were nowhere to be found, and a heavy stillness hung over the lab.

Her old station felt familiar, like returning home after a long vacation, except that the home in question was now covered in a thin vinegar-smelling film and scattered with poorly labeled biopacks full of purified or reactive chemicals. She touched the cleaning kit and found that it, too, was filthy. Leonard really was the sloppiest chemist alive.

From Olympia's station, she retrieved the original samples she had stashed from Paige's murder scene. She also brought out the samples she'd kept from Morton's death.

"Traverse's automatic full scan of material left us with uncertain results," she said to Hector, who looked lost amongst the fragile equipment. "But I also had engineering print manually operated equipment and primer so we could do some old-fashioned forensic DNA analysis. Last night, after you picked me up off the tower and brought me home, I came here to get it started."

"Finally," Del said.

Ash scowled at her.

"You realize this is what I originally asked for, right?" the older woman said.

Hector crossed his arms. "I thought we agreed that you needed sleep last night."

"Well, I didn't, because I took drugs," Ash snapped. Her eye twitched in a way she couldn't seem to stop. Ash actually did need sleep. Badly. "The sequencing takes time, but I managed to do some initial comparisons." She showed Del and Hector her pencil and paper notes.

Del frowned. "This was in the muck?"

"The muck left on the body was still falling after the murder happened. Paige's DNA was in that muck."

"But not Leonard's?"

"Or Victor's." Ash peered at the paper again. "But I have someone's DNA, so if we can come up with another suspect, this can help us prove the case."

Hector said, "Can't you just check it against everyone in the colony?"

Ash rolled her eyes. "But that's *so* much work."

"Check it against Olympia," Del said.

"What about Jasper or Gerald?" Hector asked.

Karl's voice came over the overhead speakers. "Miss Morgan, see me in the office."

"I'm busy!" Ash shouted at the ceiling.

"You can go," Del said with a hint of amusement. "We'll wait."

"No," Ash said. "Karl, come down to Leonard's lab. There's something you should see."

Hector leaned against Olympia's station and crossed his arms. He hadn't smiled all morning and Ash wondered what the problem was.

When Karl arrived, Ash had just finished loading samples into the centrifuge.

"What the hell is going on here," Karl asked.

"It spins samples really fast," Ash said.

Karl said, "I know what a centrifuge is. What are you doing with it? We have automated systems for this."

Del said, "We have automated systems for titrating liquids too, but you seem set on having Ash work pretty hard at doing that manually."

"She needs to learn discipline."

The centrifuge hummed as it spun. Meanwhile, she pushed the notes in Karl's direction. "Do you know anything about these toxins being printed in our lab?"

Karl hesitated only a fraction of a second. "I don't know a damn thing about that."

"What do you know, Karl?"

Karl's lip turned up in a sneer. "It's above your pay grade, kid."

Del said, "But not above mine."

Karl placed his hands on the table, palms down.

"This lab has a lot of goals, and one of them is maintaining the safety of the colony. Ever since we found out about the second colony, we've been preparing for disaster, and that means testing our water filters against anything they might dump into our reservoir."

Del stared at Karl for a long held breath. "Who was working on this?"

"I'm not supposed to say."

"It was Olympia," Ash said. "She was working on the filtration project long after the new reservoir filters were installed."

Karl glanced at the screen attached to Olympia's lab, but didn't say anything else.

Ash swore under her breath. "Where is she now?"

The older man shrugged. "Not here."

Del held up a hand to keep Ash from saying something stupid that probably would have put her in an even worse position at the lab. "Leonard has been printing large quantities of the toxin. Do you know if he could have stolen that program from Olympia's work?"

"Why don't you ask him?"

Del glowered. "I'm not asking him."

Karl stared down Del for several long seconds before saying, "If you have a problem with how I run this lab, you can go ahead and say it."

"Olympia leaves her terminal unlocked," Ash said. When Karl's jaw tightened, she walked it back. "Not *all* the time. Just when we're working together and need to share data." Olympia was *not* going to be happy when she found out Ash ratted her out on this. "She's really quite good at security."

"If Leonard has been making all this poison," Karl said, "then he's been taking it to the shed."

Del scowled. "What shed?"

"Up by the quarry," Ash said. "It's more of a bunker than a shed. It's where we're supposed to store things like biological agents that might potentially escape."

Del gave her a dry look.

"Or so I'm told." Ash bit her lip. "Hector can check it out."

Hector's expression went dark, and Ash didn't know why. Were they not at the relationship level where she could endlessly volunteer him for things? What did this mean?

Del broke the tension. "We should all go."

"Wait until this sequencing finishes," Ash said, pointing to her spinning centrifuge.

Karl raised his eyebrows at Del.

"We'll go now," said Del, a tightness in her voice that Ash had never noticed before.

Ash watched in horror as Karl led Del out the back exit. To Hector, she whispered, "Does Karl really always need to be in charge? What a jerk."

Hector shrugged. "He doesn't seem so bad."

"Are you kidding?"

He wasn't kidding. "At least he's not volunteering

people to go up to the most dangerous building in the colony alone."

Ash opened her mouth to—what? Apologize? Ask why he thought that building was creepy? Was it haunted? Instead, she shut down her centrifuge. Sequencing could wait.

Hector and Ash followed the others, passing Karl's office on the way. Without thinking, Ash poked her head in to turn off the extra lights and looked once again at the bare walls. The place felt empty. Unlived in.

She stepped inside and took a look around. The desk was neatly organized. The extra chair looked completely unused. Staring at the empty shelves, she couldn't help but wonder what it was like to be Karl Planski. Lonely, she thought. He was one of the first to the colony. Had he been lonely all that time? Something felt off about the room. Hadn't it once been decorated? Ash hit the lights and hurried to catch up.

The shed stood next to the quarry, its squat stone form hidden against the surrounding rock. Next to it, three parking spots for transport spiders held two spiders. Karl brushed past this and led the group through the heavy steel door. Inside sat another blast door and a tunnel leading deeper into the rock. Beyond that and a couple of heavily airlocked spaces stood the incubators, where microbiological samples grew in tightly controlled conditions. Their footsteps echoed through the stone passages.

It really was pretty creepy, but she wasn't about to admit that to Hector. "This isn't creepy at all." There.

Finally, they reached Leonard's storage containers.

Empty.

"Nothing," said Karl. He brought up the container logs. "She took them an hour ago."

Blood pulsed in Ash's ears. Olympia would have had access to Leonard's lab to sabotage his prints. Olympia had the necessary skills to print the poisons. Olympia never liked Paige. Olympia was a powerful woman. But murder? Could her labmate and friend have committed murder?

Olympia had endured Morton's advances all those years. What if?

What if?

Ash still couldn't make herself believe that Olympia would poison all those people.

Del fixed Karl with her gaze, and something unspoken passed between them. "We can guess where she's headed."

"You know what you have to do," said Karl.

"No, she doesn't," Ash said.

"She needs to be stopped," Del snapped.

"So, call her."

Karl waved off this idea. "She's beyond that."

"You can't know that," Ash pleaded.

"Ash," said Del, "Olympia has been talking about the other colony. She's been sending request after request to make plans to deal with them. She took the poison."

Ash looked from Karl to Del to Hector. "She wouldn't do that."

"She *is* doing that," said Del. "She's on her way right now and needs to be stopped." Outside, Del stalked to the farthest spider and opened the cockpit.

"You'll want the other one, Delilah," said Karl.

Del stopped, her hand already on the walker. Grinding her teeth, she switched to the other spider and climbed in.

Karl said, "The other one's got a faulty leg. She'd never catch up."

"Ash," Del said, "keep an eye on Leonard."

"Is he coming with us?"

Del waited the embarrassingly long time it took Ash to catch on.

"What?" Ash was aghast. "I can ride in the back of your spider. We're a team."

"No," Del said. "I'll handle this alone. Go round up Gerald and Jasper."

"Olympia is my friend," Ash said. "I can talk her down."

"We can wait," Hector said, and he placed a hand on Ash's shoulder.

Her adrenaline spiked and the full-on rage of panic hit her like a landslide. She slapped his hand away and glared at him. Hard. "I don't need this patronizing garbage, Hector. Leave me alone."

He took a step back, blinking.

"I don't need your help. I don't need any of this. Just everyone listen to me for once. Olympia isn't going to kill anyone. She *hasn't* killed anyone." She shoved Hector in his big belly. "I don't need your help. All I need is to talk to Olympia and figure out why she's doing this."

Del's spider lifted up on its legs and began its long, plodding walk over the lip of the quarry. Ash's rage bubbled in her chest and its heat burned in her face. Nobody said a word as she stood there, fists clenched at her sides.

"You have a job, Morgan," Karl growled as he started his walk back into town. "For once, just do it."

CHAPTER TWELVE

"You can let me out, right?" Leonard said from behind his locked door, which was absolutely going to stay locked.

Ash ignored Leonard. Across from her, sitting at the interview table, were Jasper and Gerald.

Gerald rocked in his chair whispering, "Life force times the square root of..."

Ash could never quite hear enough to know if his math checked out.

Jasper sat stock still with perfect posture looking down his hooknose at her. "Let me get him his meds."

Ash paced in the stifling room. She'd picked the men up in the lab as they pushed a bag of refuse into the smaller biolab recycler—the one they used to refine biological building blocks. She hadn't been quick enough to stop them.

"What was in the bag?" she asked Gerald.

"Square root minus the inverse of the covalent fraction."

Jasper leaned forward. The sleeves of his scrubs were too short, and the thick black hairs on the backs of his arms bristled. "You don't have evidence to hold us for anything."

She jabbed him in the chest. "I can hold you if I want."

"You probably shouldn't, though," Leonard said through the door.

Gerald's rocking increased.

Ash pinched the bridge of her nose. "Here's the thing. I know you're up to something. If that's murder, then fine. We'll deal with it. If it's something else, then why not give me a break and just let me in on the secret?"

Gerald stopped. He cocked his head as if listening.

Jasper looked to the other man, then to Ash. "Traverse suggested the frogs. That's all."

"That's it?"

Jasper gave one quick nod.

"You're embarrassed because the machine did the thinking for you?"

"We didn't know why," Jasper said. "The frogs didn't fit anywhere in the food webs."

"My microbes would eat them," said Ash.

"Sure, but your microbes will eat anything. It's kind of terrifying, you know."

"Why didn't Karl catch this? He's supposed to be in charge of whatever happens in the lab."

A huge grin spread across Gerald's face.

"He's a geologist, Ash," said Jasper. "You know that."

"Fine. He's a geologist. You're a botanist and Gerald's a biologist. He should still review your actions."

Jasper tugged at his sleeves. "We didn't kill anyone."

Ash leaned forward so her face was inches from Jasper's. "I heard you arguing about a poison. You took some from Leonard's desk."

His expression remained studiously impassive. "You want to learn about poison, talk to Olympia."

"Olympia's not here. I'm asking you."

Jasper said. "A lot of things can be poison to different kinds of creatures."

Gerald twitched.

Jasper whispered, "Gerald doesn't like to dispose of his creations. I had a way to do it quickly and painlessly. If you want to know about poisons that work on people, you need to talk to Olympia."

"Olympia wouldn't poison anyone," Ash said. Her notebook lay in front of her and nothing in it pointed at Olympia's innocence. What good were notes, anyway? "She's too smart for that."

"But you'd believe we would kill someone," said Jasper.

"You and your buddy here made frogs because a computer told you to."

"Sometimes smart people make dumb mistakes."

"No, we don't." Ash drew a long breath to calm herself, which did not work one bit. Everywhere she went, answers always led to Olympia. Logic said to stop her fellow biologist. Instinct told her Olympia was innocent, and she didn't trust Del to resolve the issue. She straightened up and walked to Leonard's door. "We need to steal Hector's spider."

The men met this with a long silence.

"Will you let us go?" Jasper asked.

After a long pause, she said, "Promise not to leave town." When they agreed she set Gerald and Jasper free and opened the door to Leonard's room. He stood against the far wall, his usual explosion of hair sagging like a deflated balloon.

On the way upslope, Leonard said, "Won't Hector let you use it if you ask?"

She said, "It's not good, Leonard. I yelled at Hector."

"People yell at each other sometimes."

She rubbed her temples, but it didn't help contain the ache. "I don't know what to say to him now."

"So, you're going to steal the only thing important to him when really your only job is to watch over me."

She thought about that for a good long while before replying, "Yeah."

The sky outside was the color of a bowel movement after a week of nectar faux-fruit smoothies and artificial protein bars. It would rain again soon, and Ash wasn't dressed for it. In a move she considered especially wise, she stopped by her house for a change of clothes. She didn't wear the yellow rain slicker she preferred for rainy days, but instead found a layered outfit of black waterproof material, complete with a loose hood and sleek gloves. She clipped her baton to her side and let it dangle low on her hip. Ash was a shadow ready for the night, and as the sun lowered itself in the afternoon sky, she made her way quietly up to where Hector parked his big spider.

And the big man was leaning against it with Simon at his side. When she approached, Hector handed his skinny friend something. A knife.

"You bet I wouldn't come?" Ash asked Hector.

Hector chuckled. "I bet you'd come after sunset. Simon guessed it would be earlier."

"I wasn't going to steal it," she said.

Leonard mouthed the words, "She was."

"Hector." The panic bubbled up in her chest again, but she forced the words out. "I'm sorry."

He stood before her, and all his gentle strength radiated from him like a fire on a cold night. With his two index fingers, he pushed her hood off her head. Without touching her, he stood so close that only she could hear the rumbling whisper of his voice. "I love you, Ash."

ANTHONY W. EICHENLAUB

She almost grabbed him right then. Almost. It was enough to feel his warm breath and the heat radiating from his body. That warmth kept her safe and calm. Right then, having him there meant everything.

Hector's fancy new spider had seating in the abdomen, so Simon and Leonard climbed in, strapping themselves into the hard seats. Ash took the copilot position next to Hector. As soon as they were in, he cranked the system up and the spider launched forward.

Rain fell in fat amber drops.

"We need to go fast," Ash said as the spider picked its way across the rocks.

"I know," Hector said, tension in his voice.

"No." Ash overrode his controls and mashed the bar forward. The spider picked up pace, its clawed feet precariously picking across the jagged rocks. "We need to go *fast*."

Hector took back control without a word, but didn't slow the spider. Under his deft controls, they flew across the broken ground, bouncing hard against cracked terrain, but never broke pace. Several long minutes passed, and Ash brought the map up on the center console.

"I want to stop at Victor's castle," she said. "If he's there, he'll help."

Hector nodded. His attention stayed on the view ahead, which the setting sun ignited with a blue-green blaze of light against the gray rocks. Ash watched him for a long time, taking in his care and

144

attention to the task at hand. She felt none of the nervousness she'd previously felt getting close to him, and she didn't know why. He operated with an absolute perfection of patience and concentration. Ash fiddled with the baton clipped to her belt.

"I want..." She cleared her throat. Ash didn't know how to talk about it, and even thinking about it triggered her panic brain. Her scientist brain took over and she went straight to it. "Sex."

The spider's feet slipped on wet rock and the whole vehicle lurched to one side.

"Right now?" Hector asked.

"Not right now!" Ash sunk back into her seat. Heat rose in her face.

Simon's voice came from behind her. "We can hear you, you know."

Oh, that made it worse. "I knew that."

"No big deal, though," said Leonard. "Never mind us."

Hector navigated the spider over a long, straight ridge, cutting their route shorter by taking a tricky route. "We can talk about this later if you want."

Ash said, "Every time we're close, I get nervous. My body tells me it's time to panic. Fight or flight. I can't help it. It's just something that happens and it's not fair to you." She lowered her voice. "I'd understand it if you left."

Now Hector turned red. "You went through a big trauma watching Marta die."

"It wasn't that," Ash said, coming to a realization.

"No, I really don't think it was that. I lost you that night. There was a moment when I thought you had died. I *really* believed it. It hurt more than anything I've ever felt. Every time I get close to you, I feel little echoes of that, and I can't handle it. Then at Victor's place..."

"You thought I was in danger again."

"Yeah. Everything in me is afraid of that."

"That's actually a normal trauma response," said Simon.

Leonard asked, "Have you tried counseling?"

"Shut up, you guys," Ash said. She turned to Hector. "So, anyway, I'm getting through it at my own pace, and I'm sorry."

He sighed. "There's nothing to be sorry about, Ash. I'm sorry I was frustrated with you."

"I'm frustrating," she said, then added, "Shut up back there," before Simon and Leonard could say anything because she knew they were going to. "So, in conclusion, I want sex."

"I'm not sure I see how that helps."

"I guess we'll have to find out." She cleared her throat. "When we get home or whenever is convenient or whenever you're ready." She was rambling, she could feel it.

The spider stopped.

"Holy hell, not right now, Hector!" Ash exclaimed.

A chuckle shook his whole body in a way that

Ash found profoundly appealing. He leaned over, paused for permission, kissed her on the cheek, and said, "We can move slow, Ash."

"I don't know how to do slow."

"Well, I hope you learn," he said, "because we're here."

Ash looked out the window and saw Victor's castle gate. In the nook where he had previously parked his kraken was nothing but a murky pool of gathering rain.

"He's not here," she said.

"Are you sure?" Hector asked. "Maybe he just sent his kraken out on an errand."

"No." What had he said? He wouldn't let them contact the other colony? "I think he's gone after Olympia. He'll try to stop her."

"Violently?" Simon asked.

"We need to get to her first," Ash said.

Hector kicked his spider up and they raced across the broken terrain. If the ride was rough before, it was positively rugged now.

"Music?" Hector said through gritted teeth. Sweat beaded on his brow.

Ash smiled. She hit the road trip mix and cranked a song called "Where the Streets Have No Name."

"Why would anyone name streets?" Simon asked.

A particularly hard bump knocked the wind out

of Ash, and when she recovered, she said, "I don't know, but having a street at all would be pretty nice."

Hector took the higher path, skating along the ridge of the mountain where the rocks grew slick with a sheen of ice in the misty rain. The sun finally set behind the cover of clouds, behind which the sky glowed with the warmth of all seven moons. The night was bright enough that Hector didn't even bother turning on the dark vision. Far below, when the mist parted from time to time, Ash caught glimpses of light plodding amongst the black rocks. That would be Del, racing to catch Olympia.

They mounted a rise, and at first the sight confused Ash. Then, she realized she was looking at a vast, still lake, with the churning sky reflected in its serene surface. The night hung heavy with potential.

And there, approaching the lake, came the stolen spider walker—the hauler Olympia had taken from the shed.

"There she is," said Ash, pointing.

Hector veered the spider downslope, skittering across rain-slick rocks. The walker gave the impression of always almost slipping, but it never slipped. Never lost its footing, even when the rocks grew long and smooth.

"I never would have made this on my own," Ash said to Hector.

He nodded but made no other response. His whole body leaned into the working of the controls. He raced the spider forward, bumping and crashing farther down and down. Faster and faster, until they raced alongside Olympia's spider. Then, he put on yet another pulse of speed, jumping high into the air and spinning to land in the path blocking Olympia only a hundred yards from the reservoir.

Olympia's eight lights shone directly at them, and Ash could see nothing else.

"Give me a minute," Ash said. She popped the hatch and slipped outside.

Thunder rumbled in the distance as her feet hit the rocky ground.

"Olympia!" she called. "You have to stop."

Olympia's voice crackled through her spider's speaker. "Go home, Ash. Stay out of this."

"You and I both know I'm not very good at staying out of things."

"This is what you wanted, Ash." Emotion shattered Olympia's voice. "This is what Paige wanted. Why can't you let me do this?"

Ash took several steps forward, until the walker stood within arm's reach. "It's too dangerous."

"I just want to make contact. Get it done with."

Ash wanted so badly to agree. "Victor is out there somewhere. He'll stop you."

Olympia's spider rose higher on its back legs, tilting forward in an aggressive pose. Behind her, Ash heard Hector's spider responding, but she dared not look. Olympia sobbed, "I can't do this much longer. I get worse every day."

Then, it all made sense. Olympia's pale skin, her

frequent trips to the bathroom, and her relationship with Simon. Ash said, "You wanted a child and now you're pregnant with one, but it's not what you expected. It's harder, isn't it? More morning sickness. More and worse of everything you've heard. That's why you looked pale that morning Paige was killed. That's why you've been wearing the baggy scrubs instead of your usual style. You're having a child like Skye, aren't you? You're afraid and you'll do anything for the child growing in you, even if that means risking the whole colony."

After the span of several long breaths, Olympia finally whispered, "Children."

"How many?"

"Three," Simon said, standing next to Ash. "All approved by Traverse."

"Approved because of the recent deaths?" Ash asked. Again, Olympia did not respond for a long time, but this time Ash repeated her question. "Olympia, did Traverse approve your children because of the murders?"

"No." There was a fire of vehemence in Olympia's voice. "That wasn't it."

"Come home," Simon said. "Olympia, we can work this out."

"What is the point of waiting?" Olympia said, her voice raw with emotion. "If we'll all die anyway, why waste time? Living this close, contact with the other colony is inevitable. I can't... I can't go through this if we're just all going to die a year from now. I can't."

The sky darkened, and another peal of thunder rolled across the mountains. For the first time, Ash truly doubted her friend and coworker. Had Olympia succumbed to the same madness that took Marta? Could the paranoia have resulted from carrying the strangely mutated child? Could Olympia simply have snapped under the pressure, murdering first Paige and then Morton?

Olympia must have seen the look in her eyes, because her spider lashed out. Simon pushed Ash aside, taking the brunt of the hit.

"Simon!" Olympia shouted. Her cockpit opened and the proud woman stood in her seat. The wind tugged at her tight mass of black hair.

Hector's spider closed the distance, its cutting torch flaring to life.

Ash waved Hector back. "Believe me, Olympia," she said, looking the woman in the eyes, "I've wanted to come here every day since we learned about the colony. It's too risky."

"You're wrong." She looked to Simon, who still writhed in pain. "The risk will be the same whenever it happens. At least this way it'll be out of the way."

"Maybe." Ash swallowed. It might be best to let Olympia go, if contact was really her plan. But if it was, why bring the crates of fireworks with all the poison? Was that the backup plan? "Leave your cargo here and you can go."

Olympia said, "I'm running empty."

Ash furrowed her brow. "Let me see."

Olympia's spider lowered on its legs, as if in resignation—as if to let Olympia step out to turn herself over to Ash. She said, "This is the last chance we'll get."

Then, the cockpit closed, and the spider jumped. It leaped high over Hector's spider, landing on the path to the reservoir.

"Stop her!" Ash shouted. "Don't let her get to the colony!"

Hector's spider ran in pursuit.

Without Olympia's piercing lights in her face, Ash finally got a good look at the ridge above them. With a scratch and skitter, another spider crawled along a higher path, only a short distance from the reservoir.

The second transport. Del's spider. It wasn't going after Olympia at all.

"Oh no," Ash said. "Del."

"Go," said Simon. He held his leg. "You have to stop her."

Ash held her friend's hands and looked into his eyes. "You'll be ok?"

Simon winced. "I'll be fine."

She ran as hard as she could through the darkening night, jumping across the rain-slick boulders to try to intercept the second transport, which she realized now must not be empty. Olympia was a distraction.

Del brought the poison.

And as the thought came, a great dark monster of tentacles and spite rose from the moonlit waters of the reservoir to strike at Olympia and Hector.

The kraken.

CHAPTER THIRTEEN

Ash slowed as she approached, pulling her hood over her head. The rain still fell at a drizzle. *Poo-drizzle,* Ash thought. Who had come up with that one? It was the worst of the whole lot, but it stuck in her head as her fingers grew slick with a wet that soaked its stink into everything.

To the south, along the banks, slippery black tentacles blindsided Hector's spider and wrapped viciously around Olympia's. Metal screamed against metal in the night. Ash swallowed a lump of fear for Hector. He would have to handle himself. And Olympia—Ash feared for anyone who dared to cross the woman.

By the time she reached Del's spider, the abdomen was open and Del had removed one of three crates.

Hector's cutting torch flared in the night, and the

spider slashed at writhing tentacles. The ground shook.

Del flinched at the clash, and in the harsh light, Ash saw a haunted look in the woman's eyes. She saw a shake in the investigator's hands.

Ash caught herself. What was Del doing out there? Were those crates filled with poison? If so, why was Del unloading them next to the reservoir?

Survival? The best chance of that was for them to work together.

All of them.

Ash crept closer, careful to stay in what few shadows the moonlit clouds provided.

"It's them or us," Del said into a comm unit Ash couldn't see. "That's what you're telling me?"

Another clash of machines, backlit by a faraway flash of lightning. Thunder rolled across the mountaintops.

"I know we're in bad shape," Del continued, "I know we're disorganized and we trust Traverse too much. But we convinced Ash not to initiate contact. If you can convince Ash to sit still, you can convince anyone of anything." Del dropped the second box hard on the rocks next to the other crate.

Ash stood tall and stepped forward. "I resent that remark."

Del flinched like she'd been shot. She took a step toward Ash, her eyes wide. "Ash, you need to leave."

"Not until I get some answers. Have you been in

on this all along? Did you bring me on because you thought I'd never figure you out?"

"It's not what it looks like." Then, as if just remembering her baton, Del unclipped it from her hip. She pointed at Ash with it. "Walk away, Ash."

Ash raised her baton on one hand and clenched her other fist. A hundred yards away, Hector's spider made the same pose, squaring off against a vicious mass of tentacles. "No."

"You don't have it in you to stop me," said Del.

Hector's cutting torch flared and Ash jumped forward.

Del stumbled, caught off guard. Ash flailed with her baton, connecting with nothing. Hector slashed with the torch, scouring a line across the body of the kraken. Thunder rolled across the darkening sky. Fat, muddy drops fell hard and fast.

"What's in the boxes, Del?" Ash shouted over the storm.

Del swept back her short hair, flinging the muck from it. "It's none of your business, kid. I'm paying an old debt."

"You have the poison, and you're going to kill all those people."

Del's baton jabbed Ash's shoulder. Ash stumbled back, but came up with her own baton to block a second blow.

Tentacles struck in unison. Hector's spider cracked. A leg twisted at an odd angle. Olympia's spider flew free, tumbling upside-down across the rocks.

"He wanted you out of the way, and part of me hoped you could figure out who the killer was." Del swung the baton, but Ash ducked out of the way. "I didn't know, Ash. I didn't know what any of this would lead to until it was too late."

Del struck Ash's elbow and the whole arm exploded in pain. Ash swung hard at Del but missed. "Who are you working with?"

A weak smile crossed Del's lips. "You're so smart, Ash. They always said you were the brightest of your generation, but that we needed to keep an eye on you."

Hector's spider got an arm under the tentacle beast, heaving it high into the air and throwing it. It squirmed and thrashed as it flew, and it tumbled in Ash's direction. She dove behind a rock, and it rolled over them.

When she came up, the world had disappeared under a torrent of rain. Del was gone. Hector was gone. The kraken—

A tentacle thrashed out of the downpour. She squeaked and scurried away, toward Del's boxes. She found Del there, prying the third one open.

"What's the plan, Del," Ash shouted over the storm. "Drop the poison in the lake and let the people die?" The fireworks in the boxes were lined up, ready to launch. She had set them right next to the lake.

One push and they'd tumble their contents into the water.

Offshore, the light of Hector's torch blazed, even through the torrent of rain. It met overhead with the writhing shadows of the monster. Where was Victor if his monster fought like this? He had to be close.

"I didn't know about the poison," Del said. "It's in the fireworks. Built into the chemical structure of the explosives."

"How can this be worth it? Why are you doing this?"

A nearby splash sent a shiver of fear up Ash's spine. Was that the crate going in? No. Deep water snuffed out Hector's torch.

Tentacles lashed overhead. Ash dove for cover, but one latched onto her leg. She screamed in pain as it squeezed her knee.

A flare of light. A cutting torch close. Too close. It singed her hair. The tentacle dropped free, and she scrambled away.

Ash slammed up against another crate, also open to the rain. Inside, rows of tiny rockets sat packed up together, chained so they could be easily ignited in sequence.

Tentacles and spider fought in the shallow water, thrashing in the pouring rain. Thunder rolled across the heavens.

Del emerged from the rain-slick gloom. "We were selected for our ruthlessness. My generation got things done because that's who we were meant to be."

"What did you do?"

"He used the fireworks as a cover to hide the production of the poison. The packaging didn't matter to him, and once those boxes go into the water, there won't be any risk of our colony contacting theirs." She sounded defeated. "I told you. Ruthless."

"Who?" Ash thought she knew, but she needed Del to say it. Needed the confirmation. Hector's spider sloshed in the shallows. The rain ebbed, and she could see the huge machines tangling once again. "This is all about the danger posed by the other colony? By Traverse?"

"People are afraid of Traverse, Ash. Absolutely terrified. Put this plan to a vote in the colony, and they'd probably approve it, but that changes us. Changes what the colony stands for. The sooner we stop this, the sooner things can go back to normal." There was resignation in her voice. "As normal as it can get, anyway."

"It doesn't have to be this way."

An expression came across Del's face that Ash recognized. It was an expression of guilt and the tremendous pressure of impossible decisions. The expression told of hard choices made poorly in the past—of people hurt because of actions or inaction. Ash recognized it well because she felt it in herself every single day.

The three crates now lay open, ready to be tipped

into the lake. Somewhere, Olympia lurked in the dark rain, ready to contact the other colony. Victor fought Hector with his kraken, but Victor had to be nearby if that was the case. What did Victor want? He wanted to avoid harming the other colony, maybe because he had ties to them. Del wanted the best for Edge. Ash still believed that, but would Del really risk murdering every new colonist to achieve that end?

Not if she could help it, but Ash got the feeling that the woman was trapped. Trapped by what and by whom, she couldn't tell.

But she had a pretty good gut feeling, and that's all a good cop needed.

She thought of the bone-shaking fear she felt every time she tried to get close to Hector, and how patient he was with her problems. But he wasn't without problems either, was he? He'd suffered in the aftermath of Marta's death. He'd grieved and recovered, just like anyone else. It was only Ash who had become stuck by the whole thing. Why was that?

"Too damn smart," Ash said. "I think I'm too damn smart."

"A lot of people have been saying that these days," said Del. "But what good does smart do you if you can't get fear under control?"

"But what am I afraid of?"

"I think you know." Del took a step closer.

Ash did know. She was afraid of getting closer. Her fear had gotten all tangled up in the mess of getting close to those she loved or those she might care about. There was only one cure for fear like this. Facing it head on.

She shouted as loud as she could over the noise of the rain. "Hector!" His spider twitched like it had been prodded from a deep slumber. The big machine started slowly moving her direction.

"You've made mistakes before," Del said, taking another step forward. Only a few feet separated them, and the rain eased to open up the world around them. "You can't live your life paralyzed by the fear of making new ones." She held her hand out, catching the muck-slick rain. "Even if reminders of it are going to be with us for years and years."

"I didn't make a mistake."

"You know you released it too early, without enough testing. You took the risk and you failed. You've set everything back, lost the respect of the other scientists, and put a big dent in your career. I offered you help because I think you're a smart kid who made some mistakes." She shot a glance back at the boxes of fireworks. "Like me."

"What did you do?"

"It was a long time ago—back when there were only twelve of us." Del took several deep breaths, then tore the rebreather from her face. "Kenner wasn't a good man, Ash. I don't know how he made it through screening, but he terrorized the rest of us. The others talked about doing something."

"But it was you who did."

"You see?" Del said. "Ruthless. I'm in charge of

the investigation because I'm the colony's foremost expert on murder."

Ash shot a glance at the lake. With the rain slowing, she could see Hector's spider approaching, and the straggling few tentacles rippling behind it. She pointed at the crates, ready to topple into the lake. "These crates," she said. "They're fireworks or they're the poison, but they can't really be both, can they?"

Del fixed Ash with a hard look. "They can."

"Not when it matters." White phosphorus would burn loud, hot, and fast. Hot enough to destroy anything else stored in the tubes, even the poison.

"We *know* Traverse will kill us if our colonies meet," Del said.

"We don't." Even as she said it, Ash knew it was true. She understood Traverse best out of anyone in Edge. This meeting of these two colonies was something Traverse expected. Otherwise it wouldn't have placed them so close. They were an experiment, and it was testing how they might react when intermingled.

"It's too risky."

"You're right that I've screwed things up, but not like you think. I released the terraforming microbes early because they needed to be released. This planet needs to change, and it needs to change fast. If it doesn't, we're all going to starve anyway. We need soil." She held her own palms out to catch the rain. "This is it. This is the growing medium that the next level of organisms will use to thrive. Just ask Gerald and his theory of life transference."

"Gerald's always been a little unhinged."

"We all have our faults."

Hector's spider plodded through the shallows of the lake, closer and closer, a few feet with every step. It became a muddied, slow race with Victor's monster.

"Hector!" Ash called out. "Can you still make fire?"

In response, Hector's cutting torch flared back to life. The dark rain retreated to reveal the expanse of broken landscape around them. The fight had crushed rocks and cut furrows into the shattered land.

"You see, Del, I'm not afraid of making mistakes. Sometimes decisions involve risk. What I'm afraid of is all the unknown risks around us every day. The people whose ideas don't quite fit my worldview. Those I love but can't bring myself to really get close to. That fear is what's hurting my relationship with Hector and Edge's relationship with the other colony."

"Risk of the unknown."

Ash shrugged. "I like to be able to calculate things."

"You can't calculate what will happen when those colonists see the fireworks."

"It's a better introduction than a crate full of

poison." Ash said, standing between Del and the crates.

Del swung her baton hard at Ash's head.

Ash was ready for it. Ignoring the pain in her knee, she stepped in, blocked the woman's baton at the base, and twisted. In the muck-slick rain, Del's foot slipped. Ash pushed forward, keeping the woman off balance. The older woman had her outmatched in height and weight and skill. Ash's only chance was to push close and keep the woman reeling.

And she almost did.

Del pitched backward. As she fell, she shifted her weight and threw Ash away.

Far enough away.

"Hector!" Ash called from the hard rocks. She pointed at the crates. "Light 'em up!"

Hector slashed at the crates with his cutting torch. Each one burst into flame, igniting a hundred short wicks. A flash of white burned at the base of each crate as the tentacles came down once again on Hector's spider, dragging him back into the reservoir.

Then, rockets flew. A series of loud booms exploded high in the air, followed by a flare of red and blue and green. The whole reservoir lit up, its rain-roughened surface reflecting the blaze of glory up above.

And by that light, Ash saw the form of Victor in his tall-collared cape. She snatched her baton from the ground and limped forward before Del could stop her.

She covered half the distance before the outsider responded. The tentacles behind her went still. Hector landed a vicious strike on the kraken's center of mass with his cutting torch.

Victor ran, but his foot slipped on the rocks. Ash was on him, swinging the baton. She pummeled him on the arms and shoulder and neck.

"I yield!" he cried.

Ash pulled the cape from his back. Then she whacked him in the face just for the hell of it. "Asshole," she said. He had attacked Hector.

Victor lay below her in a whimpering mess. She hauled him to his feet and ushered him back to the place where the last few crates fired their final rockets.

"Let them try to ignore that," Ash said, watching the sky glow with the final display.

"You've done it," he said, spitting blood. "You've killed both of your colonies."

"Better we die together than by poison in the night."

Hector's spider limped forward and the front and back opened. Hector stepped down and ran to Ash. "Are you okay?"

Ash pulled the big guy down and kissed him as hard as she could. He stumbled, stunned at first. Then, he melted into her and pulled her up to smother her in all his glorious warmth.

Leonard stood watching when she finally separated herself from Hector. His glasses were missing, and his hair had somehow resumed its explosive configuration.

"Del," Ash said, but the woman was nowhere to be seen. "Damn."

"What about Olympia?" Hector asked, squinting at the place where her spider had landed. It was gone as well.

"She's fine," said Ash. "With those fireworks at her back, she probably made a hell of an entrance."

"Wasn't she going to poison the reservoir?" Leonard asked.

"No. She was going to go introduce herself to the other colony."

"Isn't that worse?" Leonard said. "Isn't that supposed to be basically the most dangerous thing we can do?"

Ash ran a hand along the mangled leg of Hector's spider. "Do you think this can get us home?"

Hector smiled. "It's proved tough enough so far. I think it can get us there."

Simon limped into the light, knife in hand. "Did I miss the action?"

Ash said, "You're a little late."

He sheathed his knife. Sweat matted his hair to his forehead. "I was hoping to come in at the last minute and save the day."

"Day's just fine, thanks," said Ash. "But we have a murder to solve."

Hector lifted Simon into the abdomen compartment, along with Leonard and Victor. Ash took one last look at the scene, but Del was still missing. She couldn't help but feel like Del watched from somewhere in the darkness.

Ash climbed into her copilot seat next to Hector. Her body twitched with adrenaline and her knee and elbow both ached fiercely.

As he got the spider moving at a steady pace, Ash wiped some of the foul muck of her face and said to Hector, "So, do you want to talk about sex?"

From the back, she heard Simon's response, "Aw, come on!"

CHAPTER FOURTEEN

ASH WORE her scarlet trench coat and fedora, having cleaned up after their long journey back to Edge. She unclipped the baton from her belt and set it on the table, keeping her hand on it as she, one by one, met the gaze of everyone in the crowded jailhouse. "Traverse can't hear us, so we can speak freely."

"You think Traverse is behind all this?" Karl asked. "Makes sense, but there's not much we can do about it."

Karl sat in the corner chair, flanked by Leonard and Gerald. Gerald crouched near the door, the haunted look in his sunken eyes hidden behind the filter of his unwashed hair. If she had to guess, she might say that Gerald had not slept since she'd last spoken to him, and it was doing him no favors. Leonard looked bruised and grumpy, but he had a new pair of glasses that were somehow already bent. Simon, next to him, didn't look much better. His injury had earned his leg a full cast, and his normally beautiful hair still clung to his forehead with dried sweat.

Ash flexed her own injuries, feeling the bone-deep bruising in her joints. She would definitely hurt worse in the morning, but for now she'd do well enough limping around the room.

Victor sat chained at the center interview table. The gold weave in his long black hair shone in the jailhouse's harsh white light.

Tall thin Jasper stood along one wall, holding Juliette's hand. Ash didn't know why Jasper had chosen to bring Juliette from Food Processing along as if it were some kind of date, but they looked good together. The pleasantly plump woman fit nicely into his arms. Beside them, Cynthia the biochemist and chocolate thief stood in Hector's shadow.

Olympia and Del, of course, had not returned. This might have been easier with Olympia's support, but she'd gone straight down to the other colony, and there was nothing any of them could do about it.

Ash cleared her throat. "I've brought you all here..." She bit her lip. "I've brought all of you here except for Juliette, because there are some questions that need answering, and the best way to answer them is going to be as a group."

Juliette whispered to Jasper, "I thought you said I was invited."

Jasper shrugged.

"Can we make this quick?" Karl said. "There's

work to do back at the lab. *You* have work back at the lab."

"I know," said Ash. "Liquids need to be titrated, right?"

"Not anymore. I've decided once this is done you can get a lab station back." His smile didn't crease his brow.

Leonard frowned but said nothing.

"That's very kind of you Karl," Ash said. "First, let's review the facts. Paige and Morton were both murdered, one day apart, and through very different means. Paige"—Ash made a mock swing at Karl, as if attacking with a rock—"was murdered violently, as if in a passion. Morton was poisoned with an extremely powerful contact poison." She held her breath for a dramatic pause. "There's a third crime, however, and it's probably the worst of them all."

"What is it?" asked Victor.

"Someone attempted to attack the other colony. That attack could have killed hundreds of people." She addressed this to Juliette, just to see if the woman would flinch. To her credit, she didn't. "But not everything is as it seems."

"Guinea pigs," said Gerald, rocking in place.

"Yeah, Gerald. Guinea pigs." Ash opened her mouth to continue but stopped. Gerald was in pretty bad shape, but there wasn't much she could do about it yet, so she forced herself to move on. "We can't trust anything we got from Traverse. Not the logs. Not the video. Nothing."

"What?" said Cynthia. She looked around at the others. "Why not?"

"Traverse has proved itself extremely unreliable. When we first learned what poison killed Morton, the logs didn't show anything about the mass production of batrachotoxin. Then, when we looked later, it showed that toxin woven into the production of Leonard's fireworks. The compound formed would have made the perfect attack on the other colony's reservoir, if only those fireworks had been dumped into the water instead of lit in a truly spectacular display." Ash winked at Hector, who gave her a sheepish smile.

Leonard said, "Those were for the festival."

"It was a good display," Ash said.

Karl humphed. "So, there's no evidence saying if Leonard's fireworks did or did not have the poison."

"They didn't," Ash said. "Leonard's lab station never printed such a thing."

Karl said, "Says you, but where's the evidence?"

Ash took one of Leonard's hands in hers. "See these scars? This is not the hand of a careful chemist. Nobody with these callouses or these scars could have printed a batrachotoxin without leaving some physical evidence around his slovenly lab station. I checked. There was nothing."

Karl's eyes narrowed.

"Also, nobody has ever printed that molecular combination for the batrachotoxin." Ash pulled her notebook and pencil from her coat pocket, turned to a certain page, and set it on the table where everyone could see. Every square inch of the paper was covered in very clear and basically self-explanatory chemical equations, even mashed into the margins where, in order to clarify several points, she had doubled up with several different colored pencils. "I did the analysis myself, and as you can clearly see, our printers are not capable of producing this molecule. It collapses in the third stage, no matter how you do the math, same flaw Cynthia found with the chocolate compound. Good in theory, but the practical limitations of our hardware keep it from working. Yet, that's definitely the poison that killed Morton."

"You double checked these results?" asked Simon, clearly surprised.

"I'm a very responsible scientist, Simon."

Victor's shoulders shook, and it took Ash a moment to realize that he was laughing. "You are being tested," he said. "By the god above."

A murmur erupted in the room as everyone looked around to get everyone else's reaction.

"Do you figure we passed?" asked Simon.

"Nobody ever passes," said Victor, a grim sharpness accentuating his accent. "That is the nature of the test."

Leonard said, "Can someone explain?"

Ash stepped close to him. "Traverse made it *look* like the toxin had been printed with the fireworks, providing an opportunity for someone to attempt to poison the other colony."

"Frogs," said Gerald in a burst of lucidity. Tears threatened to spill from his eyes. "My frogs, they're all dead."

"It was necessary," Jasper growled.

"That's right," Ash said. "The frogs you printed were harmless until you also started feeding them nutrients similar to the insects from their native environment. At that point, their skin started producing the toxin." She held up a finger to keep anyone from interrupting. "But nowhere near enough to poison a colony. Barely enough to kill Morton."

"Oh no, oh no." Gerald rocked harder.

"It's not your fault, Gerald. The frog made a perfect murder weapon. All the killer had to do was convince Morton to pick up a frog." Ash strolled around the room, looking each one in the eye as she spoke. "There would be no way to trace the murder weapon back without video of the event, which we now know we can't trust."

Karl met her gaze. "Who's to say Morton didn't pick the frog up on his own? It could have gotten free."

Ash scratched her chin. "Right. Who's to say? He may have picked up an escaped frog, put it away, and then wandered outside before dying."

Karl nodded.

"But then I have one more thing that doesn't

make sense," Ash said, giving them another dramatic pause. "How did the frog get out?"

"It's a tree frog," Karl said. "They climb. Gerald must have been careless."

"Sure, sure." Ash nodded her understanding, then continued her stroll around the room. "Gerald, were these tree frogs?"

Gerald nodded. "They're dead."

Ash turned to Jasper. "You killed them to cover up the evidence. Why?"

Juliette let go of his hand.

Jasper said, "Gerald, I couldn't let them blame you." He turned to Ash. "I used the dose of bromoxynil-octanoate Leonard made for me to use as an herbicide, but it worked well enough on his frogs."

Gerald's scowl deepened.

Jasper sighed. "Gerald didn't realize it when he made them, but the frogs were a bad choice to release in this climate. We couldn't make them work with the proposed vegetative conditions, and the lab is short on the biological building blocks. It took some encouraging, but I finally got him to let me administer the poison."

Gerald muttered under his breath.

"Strong encouraging," Jasper corrected. "But I couldn't have done it without his permission."

"Because he keeps his station well secured," Ash said. Frustratingly so. "The frogs were killed, and only Gerald had access to them."

The room exploded with excited noise, but

175

Gerald made no move to react. Hector took the man's wrists and bound them behind his back.

"That leaves Paige," Ash said.

"Hold on," Juliette said, "can we go back to attacking the other colony? Did we ever figure out who did that?"

Karl said, "Nobody did. Pay attention. There was never any poison."

Ash nodded. "Right. No poison, no attack."

"But who *thought* they were attacking the colony?" Juliette asked. "Del?"

"You know, you weren't even really invited," Ash said.

"She's my guest," said Jasper.

Ash threw up her arms. "This isn't a dinner party!"

Jasper took Juliette's hand. "The question still stands."

"Del attacked the other colony," said Hector. "She was setting up the fireworks to dump into the reservoir."

"Someone told her to do it, but we'll figure that out soon enough." Ash drew a long slow breath to steady her nerves. She hadn't had to think this hard about anything in ages, and it was truly exhilarating. "We know that Gerald is responsible for the poisoning of Morton because only he can access his frogs, but I still want to talk through Paige's killing. She was attacked with a sharp piece of that lava rock. The shiny stuff."

"Obsidian," Karl said. "It's all over the place here."

"Is it?" Ash asked. "Oh, I didn't know that. I've only ever seen it down the slope by those lava tubes." She turned to Victor. "What were you doing down there, by the way?"

He glared at her for several seconds before answering. "It is the easiest way to walk back to my home."

"You visit here pretty often?"

"I come every few days. During the rains."

The group murmured in surprise again, but Ash shushed them. "But you have a walker. Why not take that?"

"It's nothing like your technology. If someone here saw it, they would suspect that I came from another colony."

"That's very sneaky of you, Victor." She placed both hands on the table and leaned close to his face. "But your technology doesn't fit with the other settlement either, does it?"

"No."

Ash leaned closer until their noses nearly touched. "Care to elaborate?"

"It is as you have probably guessed. I come from a third settlement. One much older than yours."

The room filled with shocked silence, but Ash didn't give anyone time to consider. "When I first heard that you were sneaking into our colony, I thought you were a vampire. I thought you were slowly taking our resources, damaging us one tiny piece at a time, but that's not the case, is it?"

Victor glared at her for a long time before his expression softened. "No, it is not."

"You're able to produce enormous amounts of biomass in your greenhouses. You've been feeding it into our recyclers, drastically improving our chances of survival, given the strained position of our supplies."

He nodded but said nothing.

"So, when you tell me that you saw Gerald and Leonard at the time of the murder, I'm inclined to believe you."

Gerald looked up, wide-eyed. "You!"

"He's the one you saw at the window. The beast outside that you thought wanted to be let in. He wasn't trying to get in. He was using the bulk recycler outside the lab to help feed us. When I looked at the contents of what Morton dumped that morning, I also saw a large supply of fresh vegetation. Varieties we don't grow here."

Gerald stared at Victor.

"Karl," Ash said, "do you know anything about different kinds of obsidian? When I found the murder weapon, I was expecting it to be black, but it wasn't. It had reddish-brown streaks through it."

"It's burgundy obsidian," Karl said. "It's quite common."

"Really? I haven't found any other specimens of it around, and I've been looking."

"You must not be looking in the right places."

"Oh yeah, you're probably right about that. Plus, it's hard to see anything through all the muck. That probably made your job as a geologist a lot harder, didn't it?" Ash didn't wait for his response. She turned back to Victor. "Why attack Hector and Olympia at the reservoir?"

"When you left my home, I knew you would attempt to contact the new colony. I could not let that happen, and I have failed."

"Do you think Traverse will burn us off the map?"

He glanced at the door. "Whole colonies have burned under god's wrathful eye."

"Great," said Karl, throwing up his arms. "Are we done here, then? I have work I'd like to get finished before the apocalypse."

Ash chewed her lip, looking to each of them one more time. She'd studied a dozen versions of this same conversation on her oldest earth media, but it didn't always work out. Even in shows where the killer always came to justice, there were always variables the detective couldn't control.

She raised one finger. "One more thing." She turned to Karl. "Do you think I should take over Gerald's lab station?"

Karl blinked rapidly. "You can have his station."

"I won't." Ash pulled her trench coat around her. "It's a shame we're going to have to reset Gerald's terminal and lose all his private research. He'll never let us past his security."

Gerald scowled at her.

Karl winked. "I'll help you out, kid. I know his code."

"You do?"

"Kid, I have everyone's codes."

Ash allowed a smile to slip across her lips. "That's what I needed to know."

Karl's eyes went wide. "What?"

"You see, knowing that someone had the code to Leonard's lab station didn't do me any good. Both Leonard and I are terrible with secrets. Half the colony knows that code, and Leonard didn't have an alibi for Morton's murder." She met Gerald's scowl with a big bright grin. "But Gerald, he's certifiably paranoid. Nobody but Gerald knows that code, and that code is required to get access to his storage."

Karl stared at her for a long time, his frown deepening.

"Did you know that Jasper and Gerald were in the Archives for an interview all day, including the time Morton was murdered?" Ash asked.

No answer.

"You read about the frog using your link to Gerald's terminal," Ash said. "Morton noticed that you changed the displays on your walls. You're a geologist, after all. What else would you put up other than a bunch of stupid rocks? That's what I found in the recycler."

Karl growled, "Rocks are good science."

"They are, and they're especially good science when you find an extremely rare form of burgundy-streaked obsidian. It's the kind of rarity that you keep in your collection where you can look at it every day." Ash stepped closer to Karl. "Every day until the day you use it to murder a fellow scientist in a fit of rage."

Karl pressed his lips together.

"It's that rage that didn't make sense to me at first. What could Paige have done to make anyone so mad?" Ash now stood with her face inches from Karl's. "Then I realized, you didn't hate her. You hated all of us. Our whole generation and our new ideas have threatened a way of life that's favored you for so long. Fear drove your hatred of Paige. You fought that morning. She stormed out, so you grabbed that rock and followed her into the storm. What was the last straw, Karl? Did she want to remove you from your post as head of the lab? Or did she want to expose how you're incapable of understanding anything that isn't a rock? Or did she threaten to support Olympia's plan to contact the other colony?"

Several long breaths passed, and finally, he cracked. "All of those," he rasped. He looked down at his shaking hands. "All of those things."

"And Morton?"

"Mort had always been a pain in my ass. We came down on the same shuttle in the early days. Me, Del, Morton, Kenner. We used to be close, but things happen. Life moves on. Morton worshiped you kids and your advances in science. Like you were some sort of gods among men."

"You couldn't risk someone noticing your missing rock," Ash said, "but when you disposed of the whole collection, Morton got into your office and helped. He noticed the missing piece."

Karl nodded. "He would have connected the evidence eventually."

"And Del. You knew her secret. It wasn't hard to blackmail her into delivering the poison once you knew it existed."

Karl said, "I encouraged Olympia to follow through with her plan because I knew the outsider would stop her. While he was distracted, Del could deliver the poison." Before Ash could ask, he said, "I have access to everything Traverse hears and sees, including every conversation you have outside of this room."

Ash glanced at Simon. "The Commons?"

"Exactly," said Karl. "Everything."

Victor spoke for the first time in a long time. "But you could not print the poison."

"I didn't need to, once I knew Leonard had already done it. I manage a team of the best scientists humanity has ever produced. Do you think it surprised me that someone thought along the same lines as me?"

"We don't think that way," said Ash, scanning the room and finding confirmation. "Victor is right. The logs showing that poison getting printed was Traverse testing us, and only you failed. That's why I didn't see it the first time I looked. It wasn't there."

"Fine," Karl said. "Things were hard when we first got here. Life was rough. Dangerous. Sometimes people had to make sacrifices."

"Sacrifices like Kenner?"

Karl flashed a sad smile. "Like valuing the colony over your own life."

He took a step but instead of trying to leave, Karl slammed Simon into the wall. When he backed away, he had Simon's knife in his hand, pressed hard against his own neck. His hand shook.

Ash watched in horror, seeing the pain in the old man's eyes. He'd survived so long on the colony and given up so much. He was wrong to kill, but nobody could doubt his dedication to Edge.

Only, this was too much.

Ash held out her open palms. "Karl, we can work this out."

"It'll be your turn one day," he said. "When the decision comes your way, you won't see it coming, but you'll know it's time. You'll see that in order for the colony to survive, for its people to thrive, you'll need to do something so drastic it'll cut you to the core, and you'll hate yourself for it."

A bead of blood ran along the knife as it cut a shallow wound in his neck. One flick of his wrist and he'd bleed out in seconds.

Ash didn't dare move. Her heart slammed against her ribs. "Wait, Karl—"

"Get back!" Karl looked from her to Hector to Simon and Leonard.

"You've never had any faith in the younger generations, Karl." Ash lowered her hands. "So, how does Edge move forward if you can't even trust us to make a decision about how justice is managed? We're the future of this colony. You either trust us, or the colony is as good as dead."

Karl said, "I'm dead either way, and if you make this decision at this stage in the colony's existence, it will affect the whole culture of this place going forward. It will taint everything. We don't have the resources to manage a prison for a murderer. I'm useless to you. I'm dead weight, so I might as well be dead." He sobbed. "I might as well—"

The baton cracked him in the side of his head hard enough that the sound echoed against the fiber mesh of the room's walls. Karl dropped to his knees, the knife falling from his hand. He blinked twice, then slumped forward, unconscious. The knife clattered to the floor.

Juliette lowered the baton.

Ash glanced at the table where she had placed the baton, looked to Juliette, and nodded her thanks.

Finally, it was Victor who spoke in his low, accented voice. "It is no prison," he said, "but if Karl wishes, he might seek his redemption in the gardens of my home, where he can do no more harm to the people of Edge."

CHAPTER FIFTEEN

"IT'S LIKE YOU SAID," said Gerald, hunched over his console so that Ash couldn't see his passcode. "The microbiome is the key to everything."

"The science committee doesn't want a problem here, Gerald," Ash said. Cynthia and Leonard backed her up on the newly formed committee. The irony of placing the least responsible microbiologist, the sloppiest chemist, and the most thieving biochemist in the group responsible for oversight was not lost on Ash.

Gerald twitched. "Karl always let me do what I wanted."

"The committee has noticed that he didn't really do much around here," said Cynthia.

Outside, the Landingday Festival was in full force. The construction crew was throwing a parade with elaborately decorated spiders, and Hector's battle-scarred behemoth was the star of the show.

ANTHONY W. EICHENLAUB

Gerald's honeycomb terrariums slid open to reveal a writhing, worm-filled wall. Every hex in the display contained a different color of worm, but they all thrived in the environment. "The microbiome is like a skeleton key for my organisms," he said. "It unlocks digestive properties in very specific ways, allowing me to fine-tune inputs and outputs for each organism." Madness flickered in his eyes. "The life force grows with every generation."

Ash glanced at Cynthia and Leonard. "Are we okay with this?"

Cynthia put her hands on her hips. "If we're not careful, there'll be a lot worse than brown muck raining from the sky."

"True," said Leonard, twisting his scarred fingers together. "But something's going to eat the worms, right?"

Gerald slid out a wall of squirming pink baby rodents. "Fifteen percent was perfect," he said. "Guinea pigs."

"That's horrible, Gerald," Ash said. "Truly horrible."

He blinked at her.

"I love it," Ash said. She really did. His guinea pigs could be the first omnivores on Sky if Gerald was careful about how they were biologically tuned. The Earth versions were entirely herbivorous, so they would be less likely to escape and start eating colonists. "I'll want to review the measures for controlling their population."

"Of course," Gerald said, suddenly very meek. Ash allowed for exactly a zero percent chance that he had such a plan already.

"What do you mean, fifteen percent?" Ash asked.

"Of your sky turds. That was a good idea, making your strain only provide fifteen percent of the material and layering in several other types to provide the rest."

"I don't follow."

Gerald stepped over to his best microscope and pressed his face to it. "Your blue blossoms are fifteen percent. Then there's these red markers at ten, a variety of yellows, three different oranges, and a green."

Ash pushed him aside and looked for herself. Despite Gerald's protests, she ran the spectral analysis on his system, finding the same results. "This can't be."

Cynthia pressed up close. "What is it?"

"The muck isn't brown because my organism failed. It's brown because my organism is one of about twenty."

Leonard said, "Where did the others come from?"

Ash stepped back from the lab station, and Gerald quickly relocked the console. "I don't know," she said. "Other colonies?" But how many other colonies could there be?

Excusing herself as the other members of the biolab committee left for the parade, she found a quiet place in Karl's old office where she could establish a reliable connection.

"Victor," she said to her little screen once his image appeared.

"Ash."

"You said your colony was old. Could yours have recently released a biological agent to scrub the atmosphere?"

"Not likely, no."

"How many other colonies are there?"

He licked his thin lips. "Your friend Del wandered in today. She and Karl have had words, but I think they will both agree to live here."

"They're murderers, Victor."

"We have all done things we are not proud of, my dear. Now is a time to reflect upon that and find ways to be better."

A knock sounded at the door, which Ash ignored. "Are there other colonies, Victor?"

"It seems likely, does it not?"

The knock came again, followed by Hector's voice. "Hey, hon. They're here."

"Has Traverse killed us all yet?"

"I don't think so."

"Then they can wait a few more minutes." Ash turned back to the screen, where Victor watched her with an amused expression. "How is Del handling this?"

"She seems pleased," he said. "I think that her experiences have been weighing on her a long time."

"And Karl won't try anything?"

"He's a geologist, Ash. He's going to be content so long as there are rocks."

"He had rocks here and didn't seem very content."

"I think the pressure got to him. He saw himself as the person responsible for the success and survival of the entire colony. Here, his only responsibility is to his science."

"That sounds nice," Ash said.

"Don't get any ideas, my dear."

A crowd gathered outside the lab. Olympia stood with two people: a slender woman with dark skin and a giant of a man. Both wore flowing indigo robes and looked exceptionally young to Ash—though they were probably the same age she was when she first landed on Sky. Olympia rushed over and crushed Ash in a hug.

Once Ash wrestled her voice back from her own rampant emotions, she asked, "Why did you go?"

"Got tired of waiting." Olympia held her belly, which still wasn't really showing under her loose clothes. "And my three little ones don't want to live in a world where we're afraid to talk to the colony next door."

"Does their colony have a name yet?"

"I got there just in time, Ash."

Ash winced. "What were they going to call it?"

"Their colony is situated on the edge of the cliff overlooking the ocean, just like ours."

"They wouldn't."

"They would. Only, when I showed up, I told them it wasn't allowed."

Ash turned to the woman. "I'm Ash Morgan."

The woman extended a hand to shake. When she spoke, her accent was long and smooth, like an ocean wave. "Palak." She indicated the giant of a man next to her. "This is my brother Harish."

Ash asked, "What did you end up calling your colony?"

Palak said, "Edge was on the list, but we call it Anvil."

"Anvil?"

Palak smiled. "We're situated on a very rich deposit of iron, among other metals. We'll have forges running within the week."

Ash looked at the sky, which was not in any way igniting into a fiery ray of doom. "Has Olympia told you about Traverse?"

"That's a problem for another day," said the woman. "We are here to make our first visit to your wonderful colony."

"Good," Ash said. "We're happy to have you." She gestured to the lab door, where she had a table set out with some of the innovations the people of Edge had prepared for the visit. "We're still trying to crack the code for chocolate, but our nectar is getting better with every generation."

Olympia gave a longing glance at the display, but said, "Actually, I need to talk to Simon."

"Is he finally back in your favor?"

Olympia put her hands on her hips. "Don't listen to anything that boy says. He was never out of my favor." With that, she pushed her way through the crowd.

"Simon won't know what hit him," Hector said.

The big man watched from the edge of the crowd. He wore a smart blue shirt and an exquisitely designed jacket that she just wanted to tear off him. With all the mess of forming the science committee to replace Karl and the impending visit from the other colony, she'd neglected Hector. Again.

And he'd waited patiently. Again.

She pressed herself up against him, straining to reach up to plant a kiss on his lips. She needn't have bothered, though, because he swept her up in his arms and kissed her hard. Her heart hammered, but it wasn't fear hijacking her body. The need to be in his arms warmed her all the way down to her toes.

"Let's go," she whispered in his ear when he finally came up for breath. "We can talk about sex at my place."

"Talk?"

"With practical examples."

"Isn't there a parade you'd like to see or a blossom storm coming that you'd like to stand out in?" he asked as he set her down.

"It's called a fecalfall."

"Poo-pour?" he said.

"A torrential brownout."

"I think I'll always just think of it as a crapstorm."

They reached Ash's little residence moments before the sky opened up and the muck rained from the brown skies. After a short time, the ochre rain turned clear, then began to fall in large, floating petals of the brightest blue. Bright sunlight shone through the blue blossom storm, and the world was, for a time, coated in the blue-white beauty of the world's first true flowering of Ash's microbes.

And Ash didn't care one bit.

AUTHOR'S NOTE

Thank you all for reading Upon Another Edge Broken.

This was the first book I wrote after the Big Career Change of 2020. Layoffs are often seen as a terrible calamity, but for me it felt more like an opportunity. This is an exciting adventure for me, and I'm just so thankful to my family for supporting me along the way.

Huge thanks to Adam and Beth, my champion beta readers. Also, a huge shoutout to my friends at SFWA and the Rochester Writers Group for supporting me along the way.

Thanks also go out to Scott Alexander Jones for fantastic editing that always seems to find ways to improve and amplify everything I write.

-Anthony W. Eichenlaub